THE VICTIMS OF RIVALRY

THE VICTIMS OF RIVALRY

OKACHI N. KPALUKWU

ReadersMagnet, LLC

The Victims of Rivalry
Copyright © 2018 by Okachi N. Kpalukwu

Published in the United States of America
ISBN Paperback: 978-1-948864-82-4
ISBN eBook: 978-1-948864-83-1

All rights reserved. No part of this publication may be reproduced, stored in a retrieval system or transmitted in any way by any means, electronic, mechanical, photocopy, recording or otherwise without the prior permission of the author except as provided by USA copyright law.

The opinions expressed by the author are not necessarily those of ReadersMagnet, LLC.

ReadersMagnet, LLC
10620 Treena Street, Suite 230 | San Diego, California, 92131 USA
1.619. 354. 2643 | www.readersmagnet.com

Book design copyright © 2018 by ReadersMagnet, LLC. All rights reserved.
Cover design by Ericka Walker
Interior design by Shemaryl Evans

To my father, Oha Nyeche Kpalukwu

Contents

Chapter 1: A Suspicious Proposal 9
Chapter 2: A Change of Heart 17
Chapter 3: The Skeptics' Agenda 27
Chapter 4: The Waterside School 37
Chapter 5: Another Day of School 44
Chapter 6: Bad News 54
Chapter 7: A Dreadful Sight 64
Chapter 8: The Exorcism of Evil 71
Chapter 9: A Legacy: The Twin Tale 78
Chapter 10: A Twin Journey 92
Chapter 11: Tradition and Trans-value! 99
Chapter 12: The Eye-Opener 107
Chapter 13: School Boom 115
Chapter 14: A New Beginning 123
Chapter 15: The Communal Spirit 129
Chapter 16: The Chosen Ones 142
Chapter 17: Educating the People 148
Chapter 18: The Send-Off Party 156
Chapter 19: Tidings of Despair 163
Chapter 20: Restless Teenagers 170
Chapter 21: More Bad News 175
Chapter 22: Rumors of War 181

Chapter 23: War! 186
Chapter 24: War Over! 194
Chapter 25: Parade of the Refugees 199
Chapter 26: The Windfall of the War 207
Chapter 27: The Waterside School Reopened 215

Chapter 1

A Suspicious Proposal

All eyes were now on Oha Achinike, the chief of Rumuachinva village, as he stood at the podium, ready to speak to the people. The weight of the people's rage, no doubt, rested heavily on his shoulders, and its effect was evident in his face and in his demeanor. Anger now ruled the hearts of the men indiscriminately, the way daylight ruled the day and darkness ruled the night! The teenagers in the gathering were restless and bubbling with energy and carrying on uncontrollably. One who was not witnessing this history in the making would have been persuaded to think otherwise, but this collective, contagious rage spared neither the womenfolk nor the children among them. Some of the children and, indeed, some of the adults, were armed with machetes and others with sticks, bows and arrows, and looking menacingly evil, as they waved their harmful instruments without a care in the world. Some held flaming woods and bamboos, while some wedged axe and kitchen knives in their hands. Egging them on, and quite unrelentingly, were war songs, some of which were made up on the spot, and some as old as the village itself—created in the days when inter-tribal and inter-village wars were the order of the day and brothers and sisters fought one another in battles over territorial expansion and bragging rights!

The elderly, in their subdued mannerism, stood motionless yet quite irritable as well. Even though the impromptu, midday assembly was unwarranted, it was not totally unexpected, for the level of the people's mistrust of the intentions of the white missionaries in the entire Ovuordu clan now festered like a sore that needed tending. The gathering was a sight to behold. Indeed, it was one of electricity, yet one starved of a cultured reverence and pageantry that was customary to Rumuachinva, dubbed Achinva for short. Anger was visible on the faces of the people as they stood in anticipation of a 'go-ahead' from the Oha. But the pervasive spirit of the mob seemed to be to act now, to get it over with now, and then ask questions later. The Arena of the First Sons, where the village gathered on occasions such as this, was filled to capacity, and many more people were still pouring in. The atmosphere was tense, and the restive mood was riveted with the music of rage and utter chaos that was, of recent, never known in this quiet African village. The day, like the people, stood divided between morning and noon, anger and disparagement, respectively, and the sun shun with a vengeance—such that could make the blood pressure of a normal body rise beyond normalcy!

As the Oha cleared his throat in an effort to quiet the crowd, the level of their noise seemed to soar higher and higher. Then suddenly silence descended upon them and he had their ears.

"*Eli Rumuachinva anu meka!*" boomed the voice of the Oha.
"*Di eli!*" roared the crowed in response.
"*Achinva meka!*"
"*Di eli!*"
"*Meka!*"
"*Di eli!*"
"*Meka!*"
"*Di eli!*" cried the restive crowd.

"Who amongst you does not know why we are gathered here?" he asked finally, and as deliberately as he could manage, while taking time to survey his surroundings and to gauge the mood of the people. No one in the crowd doubted his resolve, yet they knew that he was not one to be easily swayed by the impulse of a dejected few or a pumped-up majority.

"No one," roared the crowd.

"I thought as much," sighed the old man. Meanwhile the teenagers, in their uncontrollable swagger, were unrelenting in their noisy act still. They had suddenly resumed singing their war songs. Smoke filled the air, and nerves exploded like thunder. When quietness finally returned, however, the Oha continued his speech. "And we are here today to do something about your concerns—and to alley your fears on the matter at hand," he said. "Make no mistake," he assured the people, "we are gathered here today so we can have a chat, a discussion, if you will, on this matter that worries me as much as it worries you." He then paused a while, looked around him, as if to gauge the mood of the people, and then proceeded again.

"We have foreigners amongst us," he declared while seeming to hold his breath, as he wiped his face with a handkerchief. "Some we respect. Some we do not! Those whom we respect for their acts and deeds know themselves. And those whom we do not respect for their acts and deeds know themselves, as well. True, everyone, no matter his or her nationality or country of origin, should be respected and treated with decorum wherever they are, even in a land foreign to him or her. But I believe, and all of you can agree with me, that however one makes one's bed is how he or she will lie on it; whatever name you call yourself is the name people will call you. If you are a foreigner to this land and you have come to disrupt it and to make it unlivable for the rest of us, believe me, we will flush you out the way a rabbit is flushed out of its hole with smoke. We will make your life miserable!"

"That is right," someone in the crowd shouted.

"We all know why the white man and his friends are in our village," continued the Oha as his eyes darted here and there as though in search of the crowd's approval. "That is not news. We also know what they want from us. The question I have for you is: Are we going to give it to them? Are we going to succumb and give them what they want because they want us to, even against our will?"

"No!" bellowed the enthusiastic crowd in unison.

"Now, what do they want?" asked the Oha, who was by now sweating profusely and noticeably caught in the fever of the moment as well. "What do they truly want from us?" he asked again. "They asked for a piece of land to build their church and we gave it to them. They asked for a piece of land to build a court and we gave it to them. They asked for a piece of land to build their own houses and living quarters, and we gave it to them. They asked for workers, and we let them have as many of our young men as they needed to work for them and for free. Now, what do they want from us? What more do they want from us? What more can we give them that we haven't already given?"

"Our blood!" shouted someone in the crowd.

"Our children!" shouted yet another.

"*Chineke* forbid!" cried the Oha. By now his face looked distorted like a tied knot. His muscular, jet-black body quivered and shook like a tree under the spell of a ferocious wind. "They want our children! As if they have not stolen enough of them! They want the life and blood of this village! But do you know what I think they really want?" he asked, smiling mockingly. "I will tell you: They want death to this village! They want death to our people! But they will not succeed. They said they want to educate our children and they want to civilize our people, but is that really what they want? Look at that: educate and civilize! Is that really what they want to do with us and with our children?"

"No!" respond the crowd, which was by now becoming more and more rowdy and out of order.

"But I see more than that, my people," he said. "Yes, you are right," he said, again, looking at the direction of the "no" response. "Indeed, when I say I see more than that, I really do. What type of education can they give our children that we cannot give them ourselves? What type of civilization can they bring us that we do not already have?" He smiled somewhat mischievously and then continued. "What do they want of us? And what do they want of our children, the naïve might ask? But if you know the truth, and it is clear that we in this village do know the truth, then it is my belief that such a question will never come out of your mouths. We all know what happened to Rumuikpo. We heard the agony of the people of Rumuajor. And no one in this village can forget the tale of what took place in Rumuedu—the tragedy that occurred there, as men and women were slaughtered or stolen. But I tell you what. Blindness can choose its victims left and right, if it chooses this village we will keep our eyes wide open and turn down its advances. Let bad things happen to those other villages because they let them. Let them shake and quiver with pity if they want to. But Achinva will not fall victim to such foreign intrusion. You, the citizens of this village, are not cowards who will let strangers take over their homeland. Achinva will fight her enemy. We will rebuff any aggression from anyone against this village, and I am not boasting!"

"We are with you!" shouted someone in the crowd.

"We will not let our children be brainwashed by anyone—not the White man, not the Black man, not the Yellow man! Our children are ours. They are our possession and ours to raise by ourselves alone. We will not delegate that responsibility."

"Never!" shouted someone, again.

"We know the truth behind all these ploys," continued Oha Achinike. "We know what this is all about, but it will not work—not this time, and not as long as I am the Oha of this village. If coming to our village and asking for a piece of land to build a house and building that house and demanding us to send our children to him without expecting us to put up a fight is what the white man and his friends call 'education and civilization', we will tell them that we know better. It will not happen. Not in Achinva, and certainly not in my watch! We are not fools, and we will not fall for their tricks. Not anymore!"

"No more!" bellowed someone.

"As we speak," continued the old man, "we know that plans are being made, that plots are being hatched at that newly-built school near the waterside—the one you built with your own hands! But that plan is not for us. They are planning to take over our children and our lives. But we will not let them. They are planning to do to Achinva what they did to all the other villages, but we will not let them. Our people are strong. Make no mistake, the gods are at work. The ancestors are alive and well and as protective of us as ever! All we need to do, my people, is have faith and trust in their silent but steady, protective ways. Human beings do not fight the fight of the gods. It is not our place to do so. We have neither the strength nor the wherewithal to fight the war of the gods. And even if we try, it will all come to naught, for they do not fight their wars with anger as we do. Even while at war their anger is under control and their temperament evenly managed. Such is their ways. And such is their preference. This is why I have come to speak to you—to assure you that someone somewhere is protecting us; that someone mighty and in high places is hearing us and fighting for us! And so, my people, you have nothing to worry about. I am here to plead with you to put down your knives and your bows and your arrows. I am here to plead with you to put your fires away and drink some water to cool your hearts. The devil will be put to shame, and we will triumph over him, but not with our fists or anger. We cannot destroy a house we had built with our own hands; that is not the way things are done; that is unlike us, and we cannot act unlike us, even in this time of great distress. We must act with caution, and with and within reason."

At this stage the crowd became quiet and uneasily attentive. It seemed, for a moment, that they had just heard the word or words they had all been waiting to hear, and the Oha, without doubt, saw the impact of his words on his subjects. But he was not done, so he continued, and while he spoke the crowd seemed to hang all their hopes on every word that came out of his mouth. Yet, none showed, or seemed to show, disappointment.

"The new school is not for us!" he affirmed.

"Yes!" agreed someone in the crowd. And for a moment the crowd seemed to breathe a sigh of relief.

"They did not build it for us, and not for our children," continued the Oha. "In fact, it is an insult—an insult to this village and to the things that make us who we are. As I overheard someone say while I was on my way here, it means that we do not know how to raise and educate our children ourselves. Nothing could be farther from the truth. The parents of the children of this village are hardworking and industrious, and have always been, and our children are the example of that age-old tradition our ancestors have preserved and passed on from generation to generation. And so as it has always been, so shall it always continue to be in this village—one generation raising another! This village will shoulder her own responsibility. This village will solve her problems. And most importantly, this village will raise her own children. Let none among you therefore send her child to the white man's school. I repeat," he said, and emphatically amid the noisy roar of the ecstatic crowd, "let no one send his or her children to that waterside school unless you hear otherwise. This is a warning, a cautions warning to all parents, as well as an order. *Nkelen anu meka!*"

And that was all he had to say to calm nerves and to return the village to normalcy. It was, indeed, a wonder to behold. Which was more electric—the effect of the words of the Oha on the people or the activities of the crowed before his speech—was debated for a long time amongst village folks. Nevertheless, after the Oha concluded his speech, the crowd applauded and instantaneously lowered their arsenals of rebellion and destruction. Within minutes the assembly began to disperse. And hours later it was all quiet and business as usual in the village of Rumuachinva.

Rightly or wrongly, no one amongst the people expected the Oha to give a contrary verdict, which he did. He may have been agitated inside, like everyone in the crowd, but outside the old man seemed confident, if confidence means not letting the fever of the moment get the better of you. The expected pronouncement, no doubt, was to kill without mercy, to destroy! And each member of the mob expected him to give his consent—the okay they desperately needed to go ahead and destroy a house they had all built with their own hands. They expected him to say it quickly and with a force—such that they knew he was capable of, such that moves a crowd of people the way a wind moves unattached debris. Before the Oha spoke to them, the mob was like a heap of heads shouting and taunting one another and craving blood. They were ready to act upon his demand and command.

But, like a learned statesman, the old man would not budge. He knew better. He knew better than to give his words to destruction—a deed that could go a long way to tarnish the image of the village forever. The old man knew better than to give his heavily weighted words to a deed that could wound his image as a well-established dispenser of good judgment and unbiased justice. For, so far, he had been known for giving fair resolution to all matters he had been privileged to preside over. Yet his mind battled within him over this one. He knew that one misstep in the issue at hand could take him down—along with a village he loved dearly. Unwilling to take a destructive path and to succumb to the wishes of the mob, he spoke with a cautious optimism and a sense of duty that is emblematic of his position, vowing to cower only to reason, to the ancestors, and to God and the gods of the land!

Chapter 2

A Change of Heart

Although the white missionary, Reverend Douglass Harcourt, who had built the school, did not know it, rumor had it that the school was another White man's ploy to steal children from the village, especially since he could no longer send thieves from neighboring villages to abduct them. Incidentally, however, the villagers were sure that *Ogbueleohia*—a charm believed to have been prepared and sent to the village by the gods and the ancestors to protect the village and its belongings—was behind the dwindling incidents of child abduction, and they wanted to keep it that way. Nevertheless, rumors laden with fear abounded. But despite their fears, they wanted some kind of reassurance from their leaders, and that was what the Oha gave them in his impromptu speech that afternoon.

In addition, and to keep the intruders away, the Oha and his council of elders instructed parents to hide all their children the moment the Baptist missionary and his employed African recruiters entered the village. They also made sure that this order was strictly followed by posting spies and informants at all strategic corners of the village. This ensured that there were no surprise visits from the recruiters or their employer himself. These spies were rotated three times day and night and armed with arrows and spears and instructed to kill if necessary.

But this impasse, which mere mistrust gave birth, did not last long. After several weeks of the villagers' stonewalling of his plans, Reverend Harcourt took it upon himself to visit the Oha, a man known for ceremoniously embracing foreigners. When he got there, he was, as usual, given a befitting welcome. The court of the Oha was elaborate and well-protected. The gates were made of corrugated iron and huge mahogany planks and trunks that rose up to above ten feet. A huge cotton tree, whose branches stretched beyond the boundaries of the compound, stood at the center of the large compound, and birds nested on them. No one entered the compound of the Oha without permission. And anyone who went to see the Oha, especially foreigners, were treated with suspicion and searched thoroughly, and the White missionary, Reverend Harcourt, was no exception. Accompanying him were two Black men. One was his interpreter, and the other was his bodyguard.

When Reverend Harcourt arrived, Oha Ovunda Achinike, who was believed to be the human representative of *Agbaraukwu*, the grand deity, the village's most powerful god, was sitting down in his hut and surrounded by his council of elders. His eyes were focused and seemed to burn with rage, yet his demeanor seemed unperturbed. He was mild-mannered and rarely spoke, unless spoken to. Whenever he spoke, however, he barked, and his roaring voice could be heard beyond the confines of his large, intricate yard.

The visitors were pointed to their seats by their hosts, and palm-wine and kola-nuts were served. After everyone had stopped chewing and drinking, and the wine had been given time to sink and settle in their stomachs, Oha Achinike cleared his throat and spoke: "What can we do for our visitors?" By now all eyes were on the White man whose comfort level at the gathering was anything but comfortable, as he seemed to shift constantly in his seat.

"My name is Reverend Douglas Harcourt," he said through his interpreter as he extended his hand to the Oha, whom he was meeting for the second time since he has been in the village.

But the Oha did not reciprocate. He merely looked on intently at the White man, perhaps in an attempt to intimidate and to size him up. But Reverend Harcourt was not intimidated. He merely withdrew his hand and continued to speak. "I have been sent by Her Majesty to build a school in your village and to educate your village children." As he spoke, he rubbed his two hands together as would one with a nervous condition. In reality, however, he was not nervous. That was his style, and one that had paid him dividends in other villages, for, to the villagers, this behavior simply meant that he was not a threat to the village. He was tall and bald, and his eyebrows were somewhat overgrown. He was completely shaven, and his penetrating, blue eyes were always focused at whomever he was talking to. Yet, his voice was mellow and non-threatening, friendly and un-coercive.

"Who is Her Majesty?" asked the Oha after a long pause, as though trying to make sense of what the White man had just said.

"Our Queen—the Queen of England."

"Your Queen—right?" retorted Oha Achinike.

"Oh, pardon me; yes, my Queen, who is also yours at this time, if I may add," snapped Reverend Harcourt quickly.

"Did you say she is also our Queen? Did I hear you right?" asked Oha Achinike.

"Yes, indeed," replied Reverend Harcourt.

"What makes you think that we need a foreign Queen to rule over us? Or, are you just going around the world looking for people for your Queen to rule over? Is that why you are here?"

"No, I don't actually do that, Your Highness, and I don't go around the world looking for people my Queen will rule. That is not why I am here. However, it happens to turn out that way most of the time in this day and age," smiled Reverend Harcourt as he spoke.

"Why?"

"I cannot tell."

"Who is she, anyway?"

"She is the ruler of my people, just as you are the ruler of your people here."

"So you are ruled by a woman."

"Yes."

"And she is not satisfied with ruling over her people alone; she wants to rule over other people, too."

"I suppose so."

"She must have some nerve, doesn't she?"

"You can say that."

"And she had sent you to build a school here and to educate the children of this village?"

"Yes."

"Under what pretense?"

"I don't know."

"What would she gain from educating our children?"

"I don't know, Your Highness; perhaps for the good of mankind."

"But you are her messenger and you must know some things."

"Yes, but not this one."

"And you are also her legs and her mouthpiece."

"No, that is what I am not," replied Reverend Harcourt. "I am not her brain nor am I her mind. I don't know her thoughts and I don't know why she wants to educate your children. I am an educator and an anthropologist who happens to be a Reverend as well. I work for the Church of England and for the Queen. I do as I am told."

"I see; so you do only as you are told."

"Precisely."

"And you were told to come to our village and build a school and educate our children."

"Right."

"Why, of all the villages in this clan, did you pick out our village?"

"I didn't."

"Who did?"

"I don't know; I was only told to report here."

"By who?"

"The church authority."

"So it is the church which sent you, not the Queen."

"Well—, you can say that."

"What do you say?"

"I say both; it really does not make a difference either way."

"Why not? Are they the same? Cannot one be separated from the other?"

"Yes, they are different."

"Then who do you say actually sent you?"

"Does it matter?"

"No, you are right, it does not. But I want to know if I must let you have our children—and educate our children, eh? That is what you are here for, right?"

"Yes, indeed."

"But our children are educated already, my friend."

"Well," laughed Reverend Harcourt, "it is not the kind of education you are referring to that I will be giving your children. It is a different kind of education, the one that will teach them how to read and write."

"How to read and write what?"

"Anything."

"Can you be more specific?"

"Well, I cannot really go into details…you would not understand."

"What do you mean?"

"I mean you would not understand the type of education I am referring to."

"Have you come here to insult me?" flared the old man.

"No. Not at all, Chief . . . , I mean, Your Highness," muttered the Reverend.

"Then what do you mean by 'you would not understand'? Are you supposing that I am not intelligent enough to understand what you are going to teach the children?"

"No, Your Highness, I am saying that it is a different type of education than you and your village people are used to."

"Is your education more important than ours?"

"I don't know, and I don't think so," said Reverend Harcourt. "In fact, I know nothing about your type of education and whether or not you have any type of educational system at all. If you did, I suppose it will be different from the Queen's."

"Of course, it is different," replied Oha Achinike. "You are from another world and we are from another world. And, as such, the education we give our children is bound to be different from the one you give your children. But the difference is not my concern here. My concern here is the importance. Is your type of education more important than ours?"

"I don't know."

"Why not? Why don't you know?"

"Because I don't know what your type of education is all about?"

"Did you try to find out?"

"No, Your Highness."

"Why not?"

"Well, I didn't think it was necessary," replied Reverend Harcourt. "I have tested a few of your children already and have discovered that none of them can count, read, or write. This was how I came to the conclusion that the people who sent me were right, and that the children of this village desperately needed to be educated on how to read and write."

"Is what you call education merely the ability to read and write?"

"Precisely, yes, Your Highness."

"And what end is that? Can knowing how to read and write feed the stomach?"

"Not literally, no."

"Then what is the use? What is the use of an education if it cannot give the receivers ideas on how to feed the stomach? Is not the purpose of education to teach the children how to grow up and learn how to fend for and protect themselves and their families? Other than that, what else can be the purpose of education?"

"Well, Your Highness, what you said is true," replied the Reverend. "But the purpose of education is also to educate the mind, to learn how to read and write, and to mature intellectually and in other aspects of life."

"Yet, my friend," responded the Oha, "at the end of the day, the aim of it all is for the educated person to be able to feed his or her family and to know how to protect them against dangers and the imperfections of life."

"I couldn't agree more," responded Reverend Harcourt.

"If that is the case, then why do we need you to educate our children? Why couldn't we do it ourselves? And, indeed, why do you suppose, in the first place, that we are not doing it? And, by the way, how do you think we survived all these years on this harsh earth without such an education? Who can survive on this earth without some form of knowledge? Wouldn't that be absurd?"

"Yes, Your Highness, it would be," agreed Reverend Harcourt.

"Then, why do we need you?"

"But, Your Highness," persisted Reverend Harcourt, "the type of education I will be giving your children is of a different kind."

"Then why can't you explain it to me in plain words?"

"Because it is not something I can explain away easily," insisted Reverend Harcourt; "I am here to get permission from you and your village people. I want you and your village people to trust me. I was sent here not to destroy, but to build. I am here to help, to educate your children, and to open their minds to the other windows of the world."

"Oh! You want to open the windows of your world to our children?"

"Something like that."

"You want them to study your people and to know your ways and that of others around the world, eh?"

"Something like that."

"Then why not simply say so? Why were you beating about the bush, telling me this and that? Is that the way of your people—to not say things as they are? Now, that makes sense to me."

"Alright, then . . . ."

"Why have you made a mountain out of an ant hill?"

"I didn't intend to," said Reverend Harcourt with a smile.

"But there is one condition you must satisfy before that can happen, and before we can give you permission to share the knowledge of your people with our people," insisted the Oha.

"What is it, Your Highness?" inquired Reverend Harcourt.

"Before you open that your window, as you call it, to teach our children the ways of your people, you must first let us teach you our own ways."

"That is fine with me," said Reverend Harcourt. "That is quite alright with me. I want to know more about your people, anyway."

"Then we have an agreement."

"We do, indeed."

"I want you to listen to me carefully," began the aged man after a long pause and after consulting with his council of elders. "You see, Reverend Harcourt, this village of Achinva does nothing out of coercion. No one tells us what to do. No one dictates to us, and, I might add, we do not dictate to anyone as well. We are a peaceful people. We are like a female fish which does of destroy a fisherman's trap. Yet we neither like to be caught intentionally, nor do we like to be caught off guard. Most importantly, however, we are born skeptics. We are a skeptic people by nature, and we teach our children to be skeptics, and to always be skeptical of strangers and strange things, and never to leave anything to chance. A true skeptic never does. Because we do not know what is in the heart of the masquerade, we watch him dance from a distance. Whether its intention is to play or to do harm—we don't know, and, as such, we do not let our guards down until it has proven itself worthy of our trust.

"Having said that," my friend, "I am glad to say that we will welcome you to our village to let you and your people go in and learn and understand our people. Our culture and traditions are unique, as you will soon find out, and I suppose quite different from your own. But with open mind and care, you will learn our ways in no time. This is an assignment we are giving you, and after one month

The Victims of Rivalry

we will then evaluate your performance and ascertain whether or not you are worthy of our company. Do you understand?"

"Perfectly, Your Highness."

"Good."

"But, may I ask a question," demanded Reverend Harcourt.

"Of course, you may."

"Why the skepticism? Why the lack of trust?"

"You would not understand?"

"Why not?"

"Well, a few minutes ago you said that we would not understand the intricacies of the type of education you will be giving our children, eh?"

"Right."

"Well, it is the same here," said Oha Achinike, laughing. "You would not understand the intricacies of the source of our skeptic outlook on life. Or you may know it but would not admit to knowing it. Unfortunately, in this part of the world we have no cure for deliberate ignorance, nor do we have a solution to the uninformed arrogance of a stranger or anyone of us. And we are not fools to press you to say what you don't want to say or to admit to knowing what you don't know, for we know that some things are better left unsaid. We also know that nothing is forever hidden in the heart of a fish, for sooner or later the fisher man's wife would cut it open and prepare it for food. We have experienced life in many fronts and, as such, we know about its ways more than a stranger like you can give us credit.

"I don't understand."

"I know you don't!" cut in the old man. "You see," continued the old man as Reverend Harcourt listened with devout interest, "once upon a time a stranger walked into this village just as you did a few months ago. He brought with him a certain type of delicacy or so we thought. It looked good in the eyes, and it smelled well to the nose. Without asking who this man was or from whence he came, our people—those who were unfortunate enough to encounter him first—bought this product from this man. Some ate it immediately, and some gave it to their children to eat, and some saved it for another day. But within hours after they had eaten it, their stomachs started rejecting it. Soon every mouth that tasted this so-called delicacy died. Blood gushed from their mouths and nostrils, and water oozed from the holes the product had created in their stomachs. This village was devastated, as we buried nearly one hundred people or more. And to make matters worse, the stranger who sold this product to them was nowhere to be found. He had disappeared. Are you listening?"

"Yes, indeed, Your Highness," said Reverend Harcourt, "I am. What a tragedy!"

"Yes, a tragedy it was, indeed," continued Oha Achininke. "And this village mourned. And so, it followed that years later that a son of this village went abroad and brought with him a tuber he called cassava. This village did not have cassava at the time, which we now have plenty of and which is now our staple food. The only thing we had in abundance then and still have plenty of now was yam. This cassava looked promising, but the villagers were skeptical, and who can blame them! They had previously vowed not to trust any foreigner as well as any foreign product after the incident that I had just described to you. But when this cassava was introduced by none other than one of us, although many were suspicious, we decided to give it a try. First, we planted the stem on our own soil to see if our land will accept it. And it did. Months later, the tuber was uprooted and prepared as we were instructed. Then, publicly and at the watchful eyes of the entire village, the finished food was then fed to this man who had introduced it. We then waited several days to see what it would do to his stomach, and eventually to his entire body. When nothing happened to him, and after we had determined that sufficient time for something malicious to happen had elapsed, we adopted the cassava as one of our foods. This is how cassava was introduced to this village, and, ever since, we have treated every new idea or product that way, and your type of education, Reverend Harcourt, will not be excepted."

"Understood," said Reverent Harcourt.

Chapter 3

The Skeptics' Agenda

After one month had elapsed, and it had been ascertained that Reverent Harcourt's position and proposition was legitimate and honest, Oha Achinike and his council of elders instructed the villagers to send their children to the White man's school. Some parents obeyed. Yet others, including the Oha and a few of his subordinates, were still not totally convinced. Children were too precious a possession to just give away, or to be trusted to a stranger to train, they reasoned. And to make matters worse, these children will be given away to be brainwashed, to be forced or made to learn another people's way of life. "No good parents would give away their child to a foreigner to brainwash and change, not if they love that child," pondered Oha Achinva loudly, and sometimes quietly, to himself.

True, Reverent Harcourt seemed upright in his proposal, and has made an honest effort to learn the ways the people of Achinva, the leaders were not willing to part with their most prized possession, their children; they were not willing to hand them over to a stranger to educate. The only and most popular education for children at the time in Achinva and the surrounding villages was either farming or fishing. And no one needed a White man to teach those things to his children. A man brought up his son with the knowledge of how to farm the land and provide for himself and his family; he took pride in doing it. As well, a woman raised her daughter to provide for herself and her household. This arrangement was both natural and perfect in the eyes of the peasant villagers. Now a stranger had come among them to destroy that perfect arrangement, and the people were not readily willing to be swayed into abandoning their harmonious way of life.

Some villagers became even more suspicious and agitated when they discovered that Oha Achinike and his council of elders were merely lip-serving them and were not practicing what they preached, having not sent even one of their own children to the White man's school. Still, Reverend Harcourt pressed on, urging the Oha and his council of elders to make good on their promises. But like a guile snake among thorns, he did not press too hard. He merely pressed on gently. He had had the opportunity to live among the people, as the Oha and his council of elders had instructed him to do, and he had learned a lot about the people. Among the things he had learned was that the people of Achinva believed not only in God but also in other gods. This to him was unacceptable, and he was determined to make sure that such belief system was eradicated. However, even though he had fate in his faith and had the courage to do as he pleased, he was not going to do anything to undermine the people's beliefs and way of life, as least not now, as he had learned to give Ceaser what is Ceaser's or face stern resistant from a reluctant people.

But no higher goals can be achieved, thought Reverent Harcourt, without first achieving the goal of educating the people. And educating the people means educating their children, as the adults are set in their ways and cannot be swayed easily, no matter what. Apart from obtaining their permission to educate their children, which was not coming by easily, he was not willing to thwart established, age-old habits and way of life. He would take his time and get to know the people first and by so doing gain their trust. As such he decided to take many unannounced trips into the village, both in the day time and at night. During one of his many visits with the villagers, partly in compliance with the directions of the Oha and his council of elders who told him to first know the people and their ways before trying to educate them about his, he stumbled upon children playing under the canopy of a bright moonlight on a clear, bright night.

The night was still—just like a typical moonlit, African village night. The moon hovered in the sky and sent its calming rays of harmless light down to earth. One who did not know would assume that the light was electricity, which it was not. Fireflies could still be seen flying all over the place, but the lights they flashed were hardly visible. Yes, it was that bright! Goats grunted and sheep bleated here and there as they roamed the night, which they, understandably seemed to confuse with daylight. Afar and, sometimes, not too far away, the hoot of owls could be heard, as well as a cacophony of other insects, birds, and wild animals roaming the abounding bushes and forests. The harmony of these various noises seemed to make music for the children as they played.

When Reverent Harcourt arrived at the scene, he did not know what to make of it. The children saw him and his strolling entourage but paid them no mind, which was a bit unusual, for, normally, the children would have run to greet the White visitors. But not this time; the children were engrossed, heart and soul, in their play. This turn of event surprised even Reverend Harcourt somewhat. Usually, whenever the children saw him or any White man among them, they abandoned whatever it was that they were doing and clamored around him and called him "Oyibo pepe, oyibo pepe." But this night was different. The children merely glanced at the strangers, laughing intermittently while continuing on with their play. Reverend Harcourt found this phenomenon unusual, thus setting his curious wit into action.

"What meaning is this night play to the children?" he asked his interpreters.

"Nothing," replied one of them.

"Nothing?" queried Reverend Harcourt.

"It is nothing really," said Mr. Nnadiekwe, his main interpreter. "It is just a play."

"Are you saying that it means nothing to them at all?"

"Nothing at all, Reverend Harcourt," affirmed Mr. Nnadiekwe, "just a way of occupying themselves and spending their unspent energy."

"At this late hour?"

"Yes, sir."

"But why? Why so late?"

"Because they don't have to wake up in the morning."

"You mean they have no work?"

"No, they do not," said Mr. Nnadiekwe. "Usually the ones you see playing this late in the night are the lazy ones; the 'Weak Ones' is actually what the natives call them. They are not important to their families. They merely play and eat; that's all they do."

"And what do they do in the morning?"

"Nothing, just sleep or loaf around."

"And their parents say nothing to them?"

"No."

"Are you telling me the truth?"

"Yes, why would I lie about a thing as insignificant as that?"

"You mean they say nothing to them for just sitting around the house and doing nothing to better their lives."

"What can they say to them if they believe and know that they are weak and lazy and have neither the strength to plant nor the capacity to harvest?"

"So they merely sit around and eat what others have produced."

"Something like that, sir, yes!"

"Then we must help them."

"How, sir?"

"Now, I found my call; this is my call!" beamed Reverent Harcourt with the excitement of one who had discovered something new and revolutionary! "We must help them, Mr. Gabriel, and by so doing help ourselves. These are the people we must target to recruit into our school. We will use them to show the village and its people that power and strength does not only reside in the hands, and that one cannot contribute to the growth or progress of a household or a society for that matter by physical strain alone but also with the use of the know-how of the brain as well. We will use these children to prove this to them. But first, I want to understand some of the games that the children are playing," said the elated Reverend. "I want to join in their plays. I want to play the plays with them, learn them, and incorporate them into our school curriculum. This, among other things, will, perhaps, inspire them to stay with us and to come to our school. What do you think, Gabriel?"

"I think that is a good idea, sir," said Mr. Gabriel Nnadiekwe, who was not only Reverend Harcourt's closest African assistants and interpreters, but also his confidant.

"Of course, it is," affirmed Reverend Harcourt.

"But I'm not so sure, sir," said Mr. Nnadiekwe wearily.

"Well, I am, and I plan to use it to the school's advantage. It might, perhaps, be the only chance we have to populate the school."

"Maybe," said Mr. Nnadiekwe.

"Not maybe," countered Reverend Harcourt. "It is what we must do."

While the two were having this conversation, the children continued to play away the moonlight night, mindlessly. The play they were engaged in at the time is called ochow, a very competitive game that requires the total cooperation and energy and wit of its participants. It becomes even more intense when the groups are divided by gender, with the girls on one side and the boys on one side. The girls never want to lose to the boys and the boys were known to feel an endless shame if they lose to the girls. This competitive intensity piqued the interest of Reverend Harcourt even more, for he wondered how these children could be considered weaklings if they possessed the type of energy and strength of character they showed in the competition, and if they possessed this burning desire to win in a competition. "I think we should move closer so I can watch and understand the game better," he told his interpreters and bodyguards. But the naïve Black men were not so sure. They, therefore, laughed at Reverend Harcourt mockingly, and began to tease him about his sudden desire to learn the children's silly, moon-night game. Yet, Reverend Harcourt did not give in to their reluctance. He pressed on and they obliged.

Standing less than five feet away from the children, Reverend Harcourt watched very closely and tried to understand the game and what it was all about. There were ten boys and approximately twelve girls in all. Apart from Reverend Harcourt and his entourage, there were no adults in sight. It was nearly one o'clock in the morning and the moonlight was at its peak, as anyone standing stood directly atop his or her own shadow. Voices of children at play in other families far and near could be heard, too, but Reverend Harcourt and his entourage had chosen the Ukeeli family, which was near the waterside where his school was located, to visit that night.

The game of ochow is played between the hosts' and the visitors' groups alone. Any group, in this case the boys' group and the girls' group, could assume the status of either a visitor or a host. There are rules to the game. The first rule is that only the visitors could be eliminated while the hosts stay put. No one is allowed to cheat, yet participants are allowed to use whichever technique they know that could bring them victory. Earlier losers are given a second chance to return to the game, depending on the performance of their group. In the game, individuals participated but the entire group was rewarded. The second rule is that both the visitors and the hosts must sing the ochow song while the game was in progress. Otherwise interest from both parties would wane, and the game would be dull, boring, unentertaining, and uninteresting.

Reverend Harcourt watched for several minutes and finally came to a full understanding of how the game was played. At first it was confusing to him as it would to any visitor. Soon, however, he got the hang of it. The visitor visited the hosts, which were usually lined up a short distance away but directly opposite their opponent, leaving his own group behind him. While in the turf of his hosts, he starts from one point, either with the leader of the hosting group or at the tail end of the hosts' lineup. One by one he interacts with each member of the hosting group while simultaneously shouting the kwachey, kwachey, kwachey sound, which was mostly used by the girls or the cha, cha, cha sound, which was the sound of choice for the reckless boys. Nevertheless, individuals are allowed to use any style of sound that appeals to them while simultaneously raising either of their legs. Raising two legs at the same time is not allowed, and raising one's leg after an opponent had already done so was against the rule as well, and considered cheating. The alternate legs of the visitor and the host must be raised simultaneously for the visitor to proceed: right to right or left to left, but never the opposite.

Now, the visitor will perform this ritual one at a time until he interacts with everyone in the hosts' lineup. However, while at it, he must make sure that he does not raise the same leg that any of his hosts is raising, as they face each other. If this happens the visitor is trapped. But he is given two more chances to redeem himself. If he happens to raise the same leg that his host is raising, like right to left or left to right, for three consecutive times, them the visitor is eliminated. At this point, a new visitor takes his place. If this continues, an entire group could be eliminated within a short time, which could easily happen. Now, if previously, someone from the side of the host had been eliminated, then that person would be called back into the lineup, for his group had paid his ransom by killing or eliminating a member the opposing group.

The game of ochow is always intense and could last well into the wee hours of the night. At this particular night it was a showdown between the boys and the girls, and the intensity was such that Reverend Harcourt could not resist taking part. Timidly, he walked to the participants and asked, through his interpreter, if he could join the lineup. Then soon after, his wife, Mrs. Clara Harcourt, who rarely joined him in his village tours, joined the girls' group as well. The children could not believe that they were actually playing with the much revered White man and his wife. The noise they made was so loud that it woke up people living close to the playground. It became even noisier when either Reverend or Mrs. Harcourt visited a host, eliminated someone, or were themselves eliminated from the game.

By the first cockcrow, the children were tired and ready to abandon the play and go to their various homes to sleep. But Reverend Harcourt would not just let them go. He had to make friends with them, and he did. He used the opportunity to invite all of them to his new school. He told them that he would like to play the game with them in his new school and that he would give them books and clothes and whatever their hearts desired, especially things from the land of the White man, which he knew the villagers adored and the mindless kids would greatly appreciate. "Come to my school at the waterside, all of you, when you wake up in the morning," he said to them.

"Who?" asked one of the children.

"You, and all of your playmates," replied the interpreter to the children.

"Our parents would not let us," said one of the children.

"Then I will come in the morning to speak to your parents," replied Reverend Harcourt. "Goodnight, kids."

"Goodnight, oyibo pepe," they replied cheerfully.

This was all the interaction that Reverend Harcourt had with the children that night. Although he had been given permission by the Oha and his council of elders to enter the village and mingle with the villagers, he had, for fear of not stepping too fast, merely calculated his entry like a chicken in a new environment. But the events of the night had opened up many things and given him a reason to do what he had come to do in the village. He would use these children to transform this village, he thought and beamed with pride as he went home with his wife and his entourage of bodyguards and interpreters.

Early the next day, Reverend Harcourt dressed up to meet the Oha and his council of elders for the second time in one week regarding sending their children to his school. Soon after the usual visitor's rituals were performed, Reverend Harcourt stated the purpose of his return. It had been over one month since he spoke officially with the Oha and his council of elders. Within this span of time, he had learned the village and its ways and had learned many things and was full of opinions about things that he would like changed for the betterment of the village. But that was a matter for another day. In the meantime, the purpose of his visit was to tell the Oha that he had found the type of children he would want for his school and had come to get permission to recruit them. "Which set of children are you talking about?" asked the Oha.

"The ones you call the Weak Ones."

"Did I hear you say, the Weak Ones?"

"Yes, Your Highness, the Weak Ones. Isn't that what you call them?" With this answer the Oha and his council of elders looked at each other and began to laugh. Even Reverend Harcourt and his interpreters joined in the laughter.

"What are you going to do with those weaklings?" asked the Oha.

"Well, they are the ones I want," repeated Reverend Harcourt.

"Then that your school must not be a good one," replied the Oha. "If out of all the children in this village the ones you want to attend your school are the Weak Ones, if the ones that we know would not amount to anything are the ones you need to attend your school, then we need not have this meeting. Those nuisance! You can have them. He can have them, eh?" he asked his council of elders.

"Yes, indeed," said one of them whose name was Uchegbulem Vemehuru, an orator and a well-to-do man, whom many in the village believe would be the next Oha, should anything happen to the present one, since the position of the Oha was a lifetime appointment nullified only by death.

"Reverend Harcourt, I am giving you permission to go into my village and recruit all the Weak Ones, any of them that are willing to go with you," said Oha Achinike. "However, you must first ask their parents. Before, I had resisted your attempt to lure our children to your school because I myself would not allow it for any of my promising children. But the Weak Ones I will let you have anytime, including mine. That is not a problem at all. First ask their parents, and if they let you, which I believe they will in droves, them recruit those lads to your school. I hope I will live to see what your school will make out of those lazy souls—children whom we believe missed their way to the land of the lazy, which they had opted to be born but instead found themselves among our hardworking people. Take them and make something out of them if you will, so they, too, can contribute to society. I have no sympathy for you because you made this choice without being coerced. I believe that the gods and the ancestors have answered our prayers on what we should do with these Weak Ones among us since we can neither use them nor kill them. So I say, good luck to you, stranger!" concluded the old man.

"Thank you very much, and I will get to work immediately," replied the jubilant Reverend Harcourt. Yet, the skepticism of the villagers continued even after a compromise had been reached between Reverend Harcourt and the Oha and his council of elders. But, in the end, good intentions overcame ill-will and the villagers agreed to send only their "weak" children to the White man's school. These were children who lacked farming and fishing strengths and were almost dubbed "useless" to their parents. Their parents reasoned that if the White man could make something out of these lazy children, then they would believe that his education of teaching children how to read and write was a thing of the future—and a thing worthy of pursuing by the most intelligent sons and daughter of the Oha and the councils of elders and the entire village. But the Weak Ones, as they called them, were going to be the guinea pigs of their experiment, in pursuant of the village's skeptic nature and tradition of experimenting first and then accepting later—things that they did not understand or invent themselves!

Chapter 4

The Waterside School

Reverend Harcourt felt joy when the first child walked into his school yard. With one twitch of reasoning, and a little finesse, he had conquered the unconquerable and outwitted the skeptics and could not be happier. He beamed with pride, like one who had won a lottery, as, one by one, the children trickled into the three-house school yard. Some were fully and well-dressed, some partially dressed, while others came stack-naked. But despite the type of dress individuals had on before they walked in, the school had a stock of uniforms for everyone, which the children immediately changed into once inside the school yard. The naked ones were quickly ushered into a make-shift bathroom and given a thorough shower and then clothed by the school assistants. Once dressed, they were returned to join the group of other neatly dressed kids.

The school had three houses made of mud walls, roofed with thatches, and cemented wall-to-wall. One of the houses was where Reverend Harcourt and his wife and their two dogs lived. The second was the school house, which was a bit larger than the residential houses, and the third house was where Mr. Nnadiekwe and all the African assistants lived. Reverend Harcourt did not know how many children he would receive when the building plans for school were being hatched out. But gauging from the size of the village of Rumuachinva and the neighboring villages, he guesstimated that at least over two hundred children would attend the school, and he had the resources to support that many. But when no one, not even one child, showed up on the opening day, he knew a conspiracy had crept into his plan, but he was determined to attack it head on. This was when he made his move—to go into the village and speak with the Oha—and now that move, that little intercede, had paid off handsomely, and he could not believe his eyes!

"What is your name?" one of Reverend Harcourt's many African assistants, Mr. Gabriel Nnadiekwe, asked one of the children. Mr. Nnadiekwe is a native of Rumuegwanwor, a village not far off from Rumuachinva, and as such spoke the Ikwerre language of Rumuachinva very well and could interact with the children in all levels. He was also Reverend Harcourt's most trusted interpreter.

"Ihe-ewe-agu," said the nervous child.

"What is your father's name?"

"Ozzi."

"Your name is Iheeweagu Ozzi."

"Yes," nodded the child timidly, and Mr. Nnadiekwe wrote down his name. Just after he had written down the child's name on paper, Reverend Harcourt walked in and pried into the list of names. "How do you pronounce that?" he asked earnestly, pointing at the last written name, and Mr. Nnadiekwe pronounced it for him. When he tried to pronounce it after Mr. Nnadiekwe, he could not. But, then, it was no use, for he had already made up his mind on what to do with these song-like, tongue-twisting, African names, as he referred to them. Without giving it a second thought, he went into his library and brought a book of names and suggested to Mr. Nnadiekwe that all difficult names must be changed. "Any name you feel I cannot pronounce, change it," he ordered.

"How, Reverend Harcourt?" lamented Mr. Nnadiekwe. "How can we just change their names without their parents' consent?"

"Just pick a name in the book and replace it with their first names. They are all Christian names. We must give all of them Christian names—every one of them!"

"But I thought that is done during Baptism?"

"Yes, at the church. This is not church. This is school."

"I know, but . . . ."

"Gabriel, do as you are told!" snapped the Reverend.

"Then what happens to their original names?" asked Mr. Nnadiekwe quite condescendingly and with a worried look on his face.

"Nothing," said Reverend Harcourt, somewhat defiantly. "They lose it just as you lost yours and are now known as Gabriel.

"But that was because I didn't like my name?"

"Well, maybe these children will grow up one day, just like you did, and not like their given names. They may, like you, prefer the new names we are giving them now."

"But these names mean something, especially this child's," protested Mr. Nnadiekwe.

"Meanings that your own name didn't have?"

"Frankly, yes."

"Meanings that makes you want to keep them?"

"Indeed, yes sir."

"Okay, Mr. Gabriel," replied Reverend Harcourt, "I know their names have meaning, and so do the ones in that book. Every name means something to someone. Otherwise it wouldn't be a name. Believe it or not, even my own name means something—at least to my parents. And to me."

"But this one is different, Reverend Harcourt," argued Mr. Nnadiekwe. "I think it must mean something to his family. If we change the children's names without consulting with their families, I think we may meet with some resistance."

"You may be right, Mr. Gabriel," said Reverend Harcourt. "I think you may be hinting at something. Then in that case, let them use the new names only at the school premises. When they return home to their parents and relatives, then they can use their given names. I see that you are particular about this child's name. Do you feel the same about all the other children's names?"

"Yes, but this one is different and I am sure it must mean something to this child's mother or father."

"What is the meaning of that name?" inquired Reverend Harcourt.

"His first name is Iheeweagu, pronounced Ihe-ewe-agu."

"Meaning what?"

"Meaning: What I do not have, I do not crave."

"Interesting. Quite interesting," said Reverend Harcourt.

"I think so, too," agreed Mr. Nnadiekwe. "I also tend to think that what is in a name is also in a face. In other words, we are what we answer to. We must be careful not to change people's names and identities. They could find it offensive and react unexpectedly negative to a well-intentioned proposition."

"Thank you for the lesson, Mr. Gabriel," replied Reverend Harcourt. "As much as I think that you are right, I will overrule you on this one. Do as I told you. Change any difficult-to-pronounce names. Let me bear the consequences."

"Yes, sir!" answered Mr. Nnadiekwe. "But how can I determine which names will be difficult for you to pronounce and which will not be? As far as I know, all of them tend to be difficult for you to pronounce."

"Then change all of their first names."

"All of them?"

"Yes, Mr. Gabriel, all of them." With this agreement, and without further argument from Mr. Nnadiekwe, every child assumed a new first name. The spelling of their last names were also modified without protest from Mr. Nnadiekwe, as most, if not all of them and their parents, had never before seen their names spelt in any alphabet and could care less if anything was manipulated or altered to suit the school. It was their first time of seeing their names spelt and written down anywhere and the children could not wait to return home and share their discoveries with their siblings and parents.

The Victims of Rivalry

The registration and the makeover of the Waterside school pupils took the whole day. Apart from the uniform, which was a brown khaki shorts and a white shirt for the boys and a blue dress with white embroideries at the neck for the girls, each child was given a black, wooden slate, which was a little larger than a 25" computer screen. They were also given a box of white and colored chalks, with which to write. They were to take these items home and return it with them to school every day. Whoever loses his or hers will be flogged with a cane before another one can be reissued.

"But why do we have to give it to them to take home if we know that the possibility of them losing them is not remote," asked Mr. Nnadiekwe.

"Don't worry, Mr. Gabriel," replied Reverend Harcourt. "I know what I am doing. Letting them take the slates and chalks home is for advertisement purposes only. Children are known to learn by imitating others, especially their likes. If these so-called 'lazy children' should go home with their fine goodies, which one can only get by attending our school, then the so-called 'strong ones' will begin to question their parents' judgment."

"Is that what you want?"

"For the children to question their parents' judgment, you mean?"

"Yes."

"Of course, that is what I want, Mr. Gabriel," answered Reverend Harcourt. "Once that begins to happen, this place will be flooded with new faces, new pupils wanting to register for school."

"But we don't have that much room."

"Then we will make more."

"How?"

"Leave that to me, Mr. Gabriel," snapped Reverend Harcourt. "Worry only about your work as an assistant and an interpreter. Let me worry about the administration and where the money and the resources for the school will come from. You have never been to England and you don't know what the English have. England is very rich, and the Queen and the church command a lot of wealth. What it will take to cater to these children, no matter their number, is only a drop in the bucket. Besides, their parents pay taxes. It is their own tax money that will be used to educate them and make their lives better. I know what you are thinking, but let us not kid ourselves. You know how long it took me to convince those villagers to let their children come here. As you know, that was a feat. Do you hear me? Now, how many of them came on the opening day?"

"None."

"That is right, none."

"Why do you think that was?" asked Mr. Nnadiekwe.

"Because they are set in their ways and never want to change," said Reverend Harcourt. "They do not yet see the wave of change coming their way. And I bet you, it will sweep them off their feet before they realize it. And by that time I may not even be around to witness it, and it may come too late for them. It may be that they will be taken unawares, not because they were not informed, but because they heard but failed to heed."

"But can you blame them?"

"No, I do not blame them. In fact, I do not blame anybody," said Reverend Harcourt. "Yet I believe that a little mind opening can do them a whole lot of good. I can bet you anything, based on the resistance we received, that no new child will join those children; none, not the ones their parents' consider as treasures and keepers of the village tradition. But I am not worried. I am not worried at all. I believe that I can work with the so-called 'weak ones' and transform them into the 'strong ones'. Believe it or not, Mr. Gabriel, these so-called 'weak ones' will be the future makers of this village, not the farmers and the fishers and the dancers and the wrestlers. The future of this village will be in the hands of these ones that live the life of boredom as burdens and are seen as such, a burden to their families and to society. Just as their parents feel happy and relieved that they have sent them to me, so will they feel happy and joyous when I return them happy and transformed, mentally and physically. Now, Mr. Gabriel, do you like the fact that they label them 'lazy' and 'weak'?"

"No, not at all," replied Mr. Nnadiekwe. "But that is how our people are. If you cannot farm and do not have the strength to either fish or trap animals, they consider you lazy. But to be fair to them, however, those are the only things we know how to do. There are no other professions out there that one can pursue and make money to feed one's family. Wrestlers do not earn money. Musicians do not earn money. And artists do not earn money. They are merely considered treasures of the village, and they exist mainly to entertain the village and to be admired and appreciated. And no matter how involved they are in their 'naturally-gifted pastimes' they must also know how to farm and fish. Otherwise their families will starve. That is how it is and, as such, I don't blame parents who insist that their children become proficient in fishing and farming, whether they are good at it or not."

"So labeling the children and stigmatizing them as 'lazy' or 'weak' is good," asked Reverend Harcourt.

"No, I don't think so. And that is not what I mean. But what can we do. We live in a society that label people. And once you are labeled, whether you like it or not, you become that which they have labeled you."

"True," replied Reverend Harcourt. "And that is what worries me, Mr. Gabriel, even though I know it is the same everywhere in the world. Not just here. Labeling amounts to stigmatizing. But I tell you what, all that name calling and labeling will change once these children begin to show exactly what they are truly made of. It is clear that they are not made for fishing and farming and dancing and wrestling. It is my belief that they were brought to this world to fulfill certain purposes. Every human being was. And I really believe that these children are no exception. I really do. As they say, 'the stone that the builders refused will one day become the head corner stone.' These children will prove how true that saying really is. Mark my words!"

Chapter 5

Another Day of School

When the pupils returned to school the next day and no new faces returned with them, Reverend Harcourt was not surprised. His assistants, especially Mr. Gabriel Nnadiekwe, however, were shocked. But their shock and awe was not because no new faces showed up, but because Reverend Harcourt was right in his prediction of the outcome. They could not believe that he could have, within a few years of residence among them, mastered the ways of the natives enough to give such an accurate prediction of their reactions. What they did not know was that Reverend Harcourt was both a psychologist and an anthropologist and had over the years read a lot about what to expect and what not to expect from native peoples everywhere. His arrays of experience in his studies and in dealing with native peoples around the world had armed him with a rare gift of being able to read people and ascertain their mindset either remotely or while sitting face to face with them.

This state of perplexity at what the White man can and cannot do raised a lot of questions in the minds of the assistants. In fact, it made them uneasy around the man they have been working with for several years now and have been accustomed to all these years. Yet, there was something about the way he made this prediction

The Victims of Rivalry

that raised the eyebrows of his assistants, which prompted them to begin asking questions.

"Are you psychic?" asked Mr. Nnadiekwe.

"No, I am an Anthropologist, I told you many times."

"What is that?"

"Studies of native peoples and things of antiquity."

"So, what they said of you and all the White people is true."

"Who are they?"

"No one—just friends."

"And what did they say of 'us' White people?"

"They say all of you are psychic and can predict the future and read minds, too."

"That is not true," said Reverend Harcourt, with a smile.

"But yesterday you told us that no new faces would come and today none came. If you can predict something like that and it comes true, doesn't that make you a psychic?"

"No, it does not. But it does mean that my studies and all the experience I have gained over the years in dealing with native peoples all over the world, and particularly in Africa, are paying off handsomely. Now, I cannot take for granted such an experience if the truth about what to expect were not clear to me.

"You see, Mr. Gabriel," continued Reverend Harcourt, "the native peoples do not mince their words, I know you know that, and I have been here long enough to realize that. They do not say one thing and do another. That is one thing I have learned about them. So when they tell me something, I know it is coming from their hearts. I do not expect anything else other than what they told me. So when they told me that they will be sending only the 'weak ones' amongst their children, I believed them. These people know the true meaning of a person's word being his or her bond. They practice that saying; they live that saying. Their so-called 'weak' children may have come home with all the things we gave them, and you would think that that would sway their parents to change their minds and let the rest of their children come so they, too, can get those things, but they would not. Do you know why?"

"No, I do not know," replied Mr. Nnadiekwe.

"But you must know; they are your people and you are one of them."

"Yes, they are my people, but I don't know how you could have predicted them so well when even I could not."

"Because I believe that they have something that ticks in their blood that is rare to find anywhere. There is one thing that runs through the blood of every native people I have met as I study them around the world."

"What is that?"

"Pride."

"You are right."

"You bet, I am. They give you their word, and they stick to it. It does not matter the circumstances. Believe it or not, that is what I like about them."

"Why?"

"The fact that I can predict them."

"Is that a good thing or a bad thing?"

"For who?"

"For both."

"Well, for me, it is a good thing. It means that there are no surprises when dealing with them. What you see is what you get. I don't think it can get any better than that for a stranger in a foreign land. It gives me confidence and assures me that I cannot falter if I stick to the script."

"And for them?"

"What do you mean?"

"What do they gain for being so direct and so predictable?"

"For them, Oh, Mr. Gabriel," said Reverend Harcourt, laughing, "I am not so sure. You see, rigidity in anything tends to give your secrets away. Being that others can predict you because you are set in your ways and will not change it, ever, creates a sense of vulnerability. If people know that you go to bed at ten o'clock every day and will never miss a day, they will not plan to attack you at nine or eight o'clock. Instead they will come after ten o'clock, when

The Victims of Rivalry

they know you are sound asleep. But if you give people a sense of flexibility in your schedule, it will be hard for them to predict you because they don't know whether you are asleep or awake.

"The villagers are set in their ways, and they will never change it for anything. That is what I have learned over the years. And that is why I can predict them so well, not because I am a psychic. I am not; I'm just a good observer. And talking of observation, what, Mr. Gabriel, have you observed among our pupils?"

"Regarding to what?"

"Their willingness to learn and to be here with us."

"It is hard to say at this time, Reverend Harcourt," replied Mr. Nnadiekwe. "Some of them are quite old and past the age of learning the alphabets, and, as you said, some are set in their ways. I believe that we will have a hard time convincing those. Yet there are those who are young and have let their curious minds loose. Those, I believe, are promising."

"Then you must separate them."

"Why?"

"Because we need results; we need to convince the villagers that education is a good thing for their children, not just the 'weak ones."

"But what has that to do with separating them."

"Once they are separated, then we can teach the quick-minded ones at a faster pace, and the others at a slower pace."

"Okay, I see what you mean."

"And do you think it is a good idea?"

"Yes, I believe so."

"Good. Then let's do it."

"Yes, sir," said Mr. Nnadiekwe. "But before we go on, I have a question."

"Then ask me."

"Sir, if you are a psychologist and an anthropologist, then why are you a

Reverend?"

"Oh, Mr. Gabriel, you are still there," replied Reverend Harcourt. "Gabriel, forget about that; let us move on. Let us move past that, shall we? It is a long story and I don't have time for that now. We have much work on our hands than to sit here and talk about me or you. Let us keep that conversation for another day—perhaps a day when we are less busy. These children need us, and this village needs us more. There will have to be some changes in how we deal with the pupils and the village as well. How to go about making those changes is what should preoccupy our minds, nothing else."

This was the conversation Reverend Harcourt and his assistant, Mr. Nnadiekwe, had that led them in the path of deciding to change the village of Rumuachinva for the better! It was a plan that Reverend Harcourt had carefully hatched out from the first day he stepped his foot on the village. But it will be a daunting task, and one that will bring them face to face with the wrath of the "gods" of the land. For Mr. Nnadiekwe, the predicted changes should occur at the Waterside school and then slowly sip into the village via the pupils. And that was what he suggested to Reverend Harcourt. This path, to him, was more manageable and achievable. To Reverend Harcourt, however, boldly challenging the natives to abandon their old ways was what was in the forecast, and he was not going to waver for any reason.

By the end of the first month of the schools inception, just when the new plan was being put into action, and contrary to Reverend Harcourt's prediction, the school had swelled to well more than two hundred pupils. More teachers and assistants had been recruited, and new buildings were being erected to house them all, both the students and the teachers and the assistants, some of whom were foreign or from neighboring villages.

As far as Reverend Harcourt could see, things were looking well for the Waterside school, and its bright future was almost guaranteed. It also meant that it was time for him to make his move by implementing his second agenda in his bid to reshape the minds of the people of Rumuachinva. It so happened that during the period he was canvassing the village and studying them as the Oha and his council of elders had demanded of him, he had come across a group of mourners. These people were mainly women and children. They were crying and wailing as they trudged behind a group of men carrying what looked like logs wrapped in cloths. The Reverend did not know what it was that the men were carrying. But when he asked his assistants, one of them inquired from the natives and was told one of the most amazing tales that the Reverend had never heard in his lifetime.

"Why are the women wailing?" inquired Reverend Harcourt.

"I don't know, but I think I have an idea," replied Mr. Nnadiekwe, who was aware of the native cultures and knew exactly what was amiss because the same practice occurs in his village of Rumuegwanwor. "If I am not mistaking, I think they are crying about what the men are carrying on their heads?"

"What are the men carrying on their heads?" asked Reverend Harcourt.

"Children."

"What do you mean?"

"Yes, they are carrying children, twins or *ijima, as our people call them*," he added.

"Are they dead?"

"No, they are not; I don't think so."

"Then why are they wrapped up in such a manner."

"To suffocate them before they reach the Evil Forest."

"Suffocate them?" fumed Reverend Harcourt. "What are you talking about? What is Evil Forest?"

"Reverend Harcourt," replied Mr. Nnadiekwe, "twins or *ijima*, as they are called around here, are forbidden in this clan. No woman is supposed to conceive twins; in short, it is considered an abomination to conceive twins in this land."

"Why?"

"That is the belief in this village and throughout Ovuordu clan."

"So those men are carrying live children."

"Yes."

"Then we must rescue them."

"Rescue who?" inquired Mr. Nnadiekwe.

"The children."

"No, Reverend Harcourt," replied Mr. Nnadiekwe, vehemently, "those men will kill us if we try."

"Then so be it; we must rescue those children," insisted Reverend Harcourt. "Twins are a blessing to the parents and to the world. For God's sake, who in the world told them that twins are a curse? A curse to who?"

"I don't know."

"So do you think they are dead?"

"I am sure they must be dead by now; perhaps they are not," replied Mr. Nnadiekwe, hoping his initial answer, which was a lie, would dissuade the Reverend. But it did not.

"Well, let's go and find out," retorted Reverend Harcourt. And with these few words, he walked bravely past the wailing woman and straight to the men and asked: "What are you carrying?"

"*Ijima*," replied one of the men. "That woman," the man pointed at a woman crying uncontrollably, "had given birth to *ijima* and that is an abomination in this land. It is an insult and a curse to this land. To remove such a curse, we must take the two children to the Evil Forest. That way no one will be harmed."

"But the children are harmed," cried Reverend Harcourt.

"Yes," replied the man, "because they are evils, and death is what they deserve for ever being born evil. The Evil Forest is where we take evil people, including twins."

"You must be kidding me," said an alarmed Reverend Harcourt.

"No, I am telling you the truth," replied the man affirmatively through the interpreter, Mr. Nnadiekwe, as the procession continued.

"So how long has this practice been going on?"

"Ever since this village was founded; in fact, this tradition is practiced not only in our village but in the surrounding villages as well. Throughout Ovuordu."

"But, is it a good practice?"

"How will I know?"

"Can you kindly deliver the children to me instead of sending them to the Evil Forest."

"No, *Chineke* forbid!" replied the men.

"Why not?"

"Then the curse will be on us. Then the wrath of *Ohiomini* will be upon this village."

"Who is *Ohiomini*?"

"The Evil Forest," answered Mr. Nnadiekwe.

"No, the wrath will be upon me, not upon you and not upon the village," insisted Reverend Harcourt.

"So you want the wrath of *Ohiomini* to come upon you," asked the men in astonishment.

"Yes," replied Reverend Harcourt.

"Then you must be insane."

"No, I am not," said Reverend Harcourt. "I mean it. Let me have the children."

"If you really want them," said one of the men, "then you must wait until we have delivered them to *Ohiomini*. After we had put them there, then you can take your own hands, pick them up, and take them with you to your house. That way our hands are off."

"Yes, I agree, I will do that," replied Reverend Harcourt. But Mr. Nnadiekwe would not go along. He adamantly told Reverend Harcourt that he will not go along with him and the men to the forest of evils. Yet, this weak-knee reaction from Mr. Nnadiekwe did not deter Reverend Harcourt. "Get behind me, Satan!" he spat disdainfully. The Reverend knew that he was right and that the people surrounding him were wrong. He was determined to prove his rightness to them. With this resolve, he followed the men to the Evil Forest. After they had reached the limits of the village of Achinva, the wailing women, including the twins' mother, receded, but the procession of the men continued, and tagging alongside them was the "fearless" White man, Reverend Harcourt. The scenario amused the men somewhat, but they did not utter a word or try to discourage him further. They merely let him follow them, unsure of what his real intentions were.

When they reached the entrance of the Evil Forest, they all filled into the narrow path that led to the heart of it and Reverend

Harcourt followed, budding last. By the time they got nearer to where the children would be deposited, the stench of dead corpses was unbearable. It was even worse for Reverend Harcourt, who had never before in his life seen anything like it, but he was determined to go through with his plans. While the men were walking, they came across well-fed leopards and other wildcats and other corpse-eating animals, which were devouring dead corpses and paying them no mind. Finally, the men selected a spot, dug a small hole, and deposited the two twins and quickly embarked on their return home. But no sooner than they buried the twins than Reverend Harcourt bravely scooped them up and followed the men from behind. The men became afraid; they feared what might happen to a human being who had boldly taken food out of the mouth of a god as powerful as *Ohiomini*. As a result, they ran, leaving Reverend Harcourt alone in the heart of the forest. But Reverend Harcourt was not afraid and neither was he discouraged. He had nothing to go by to be afraid. He had no knowledge of the wrath of *Ohiomini* and could care less what these people were thinking. So he merely picked up the two twins and began to unwrap the clothes that were used to suffocate them. But by now they were all dead—the two of them. Yet, despite that they were dead, the Reverend decided to take their dead corpses home anyway, having decided to give them a proper, Christian burial!

When the natives saw Reverend Harcourt, they came out in droves, terribly afraid, wondering what might happen to him for taking food out of the mouth of a powerful god like *Ohiomini,* who was one of the most feared among the gods due to his wrathful reaction whenever provoked. A multitude of the villagers thronged to Reverend Harcourt's Waterside school and hung around the school yard to see what would happen to him.

When the assistants, including Mr. Nnadiekwe, saw what Reverend Harcourt had done, they feared that his days were numbered. But Reverend Harcourt was not perturbed. He simply told one of his laborers to dig two four feet holes in front of his house and told another to make two makeshift caskets. After the holes had been dug and the caskets made, he brought out the corpses of the dead twins, deposited them in the caskets and told his assistants to bury them. But before they buried them, he prayed for them, read a passage or two from the Bible and asked God to bless the twins and to give them a better life elsewhere, where they would be appreciated and let live!

Chapter 6

Bad News

The news of what Reverend Harcourt had done quickly spread throughout the village of Rumuachinva and beyond. But the natives were not amused, especially the Oha and his council of elders. They saw the act of a foreigner coming to their village and challenging the gods of their land as a challenge to them, not to the gods. They reckoned that it was they, the rulers of the land, who had permitted this foreigner to live amongst them. And now he had gained enough strength that he had begun to take matters into his own hands. He no longer respected them, and he no longer respected their gods. As such, they were not amused. But they must act quickly to diffuse the situation so that he does not bring more shame to them. They must call him to their means and ask on whose authority he had done what he did. But first, they must visit the shrine of *Ohiomini* to clear their names and ask the god to go after the one who had defiled him by forcibly taking food out of his mouth.

After they had performed the appeasement rituals and had confirmed that the god had accepted their plea for pardon on what had taken place, the Oha and his council of elders sent for Reverend Harcourt, urging the messenger to tell him to come to the court of the Oha first thing the next day. When the messenger arrived at the Waterside school, he was surprised the see that the parents of the pupils had not asked their children to stay away from a man who had offended *Ohiomini* and would soon fall into the axe of the bloodthirsty god himself. The school was operating as usual and Reverend Harcourt was going about his normal duties without worry.

"Tell them I will see them first thing tomorrow morning," he had replied the messenger, who, in turn, returned quickly to convey Reverend Harcourt's reply to the Oha and his council of elders.

"Did you find him in good health?" asked the Oha.

"Yes," replied the messenger, "he seemed quite fine and unperturbed, to say the least."

"I am surprised," replied one of the elders.

"I am not," said another.

"Why not?"

"Well, I have heard so much news about those White people."

"What type of news?" asked Oha Achinike.

"Well, I have heard that they are spirits themselves and can commune with spirits."

"Did you also hear that they can offend the spirits the way that man had offended *Ohiomini*?" asked the Oha. "One thing is being able to commune with the spirits and another thing is offending them so openly as this man had done. I commune with spirits all the time myself, but do I challenge them? Of course, not. I don't think *Ohiomini* will take this challenge lying down. No, *Ohiomini* is not that passive when offended, not at all. And I don't think this man will get away with what he had done. Let us just wait and see."

"You are right; let us wait and see," said Uchegulem Vemehuru, one of the elders. "It is not our place to fight the war of the gods. I believe that the gods are wise and strong enough to fight their own war. We only do their bidding. This particular situation is out of our hands and quite above us. But we must not rush to judgment. We must wait to hear on whose authority this White man had done what he did. If he has a charm, we must know. If he has a god behind him, we must know. And if his god is stronger than our own gods, we will also find out."

"Amen!" shouted Uzor Wagbara, the chief priest of *Ohiomini*, who was fuming and was feeling deeply offended by what had happened to *Ohiomini* under his watch. His reasons for feeling this way were numerous. One, and perhaps the most prominent, is that he would be seen as someone presiding over a powerless god, and he would rather die than accept that notion.

Several months passed without any incidents, and for a while it seemed as though the Reverend had defeated a god. As expected, people had begun raising eyebrows and wondering about the truth behind the invincible powers of the gods. A few days into the seventh month, however, Reverend Harcourt arrived at the palace of the Oha with tears in his eyes. The moment he entered the hut where the Oha and his council of elders were seated, he fell on the ground and cried hysterically. Mr. Gabriel Nnadiekwe, his most trusted assistant and confidant was with him, and even *he* could not restrain his own tears. This behavior startled everyone present, including those who had prematurely accorded the White man the status of a god, for they could not imagine him crying. They did not know what to make of it, as neither Reverend Harcourt nor Mr. Nnadiekwe were talking. They merely sobbed and aggrieved until Mr. Nnadiekwe stopped sobbing and began pleading with the Oha and his council of elders: "We need your help, great father," he pleaded. "Quickly, we need your help. She is dead. The White man's wife is dead."

"*Aya!*" shouted Chief Wagbara.

"What did you say, young man?" asked Oha Achinike.

"Mrs. Harcourt is dead. She fell down on the ground and died this morning," repeated Mr. Nnadiekwe.

"Why are you lying?" questioned one of the elders.

The Victims of Rivalry

"No, I am not lying," said Mr. Nnadiekwe. "She is really dead and we need your help. That is what Reverend Harcourt had come for, not because you had asked him to come as he had promised to come this morning. He had come to ask for your help to revive her."

"*Aya!*" repeated Chief Wagbara. "Tell him we do not revive the dead. Tell him that he had offended the worst of them all and he will pay. Tell him this is just the beginning and more bad things are on the way. Tell him that no one had ever offended *Ohiomini* and gotten away with it. Tell him that *Ohiomini* fights his own war and is prepared to fight and finish whoever provokes him. Tell him he had called the wrath of the Evil Forest upon himself and he alone must bear the consequences of the god of *Okporo*."

"Stop! Speak no more," said Oha Achinike, to the chief priest of *Ohiomini*, Chief Wagbara, who seemed carried away with his lamentation of the powers of *Ohiomini*. "Now, cry no more and tell us what had happened," said the Oha to Mr. Nnadiekwe. "If I heard you right, did you say that the wife of the White man is dead?"

"Yes, she is dead."

"Are you sure she is not sleeping."

"Yes, I am sure."

"How did she die?"

"She woke up this morning. I saw her. Nothing was wrong with her. Then she suddenly fell on the ground, face first, and died on the spot. Her husband and I tried everything we could to revive her but we could not. That is why we came here to seek your help. Perhaps you might help. Please send someone to help us appease the gods. Maybe the gods had done it. Maybe the wrath of the gods had killed her."

"Young man, hush your mouth," responded Oha Achinike, "we don't know that yet. Now, tell the White man to go. Let us see what we can do."

"What can we do?" shouted Chief Wagbara. "There is nothing we can do. He offended *Ohiomini* and he paid the ultimate price. That is what he deserves. Next time he will stay away from things that do not concern him. Next time he will keep to himself and leave others alone."

"Enough!" said Oha Achinike to Chief Wagbara. "Let us send people to go and help our visitor. Uzor, I want you and a group of men to go to the Waterside school and see what you can do to help our visitor. Bring us report as quickly as possible. When you go there do what is right. Do not let your mouth do all the work? A mature man is supposed to control his mouth. You are supposed to do the biddings of the gods, not speak or act for them."

With this admonishment by Oha Achinike, Chief Wagbara and his men rushed quickly to the Waterside school. When they got there, Reverend Harcourt and his assistants were still crying. Meanwhile, they had picked up Mrs. Harcourt and laid her face-up on her bed, covered her body, and left her face open.

"Where is she?" asked Chief Wagbara.

"Inside," replied Mr. Nnadiekwe.

"Didn't you say she fell face-down?"

"Yes, she fell face-down on the ground and stopped breathing almost immediately."

"Then, where is she?"

"She is inside; we picked her up and laid her in her bed."

"You picked her up?"

"Yes, we did. Something wrong with that?"

"Then we can't help you," shouted Chief Wagbara. "You are from this area, young man, are you not?

"Yes, I am," replied Mr. Nnadiekwe.

"And you know our customs and traditions?"

"Yes, I do."

"And you know you are not supposed to pick her up without sacrifices."

"What do you mean?"

"That is against the law of this land?"

"What is against the law?"

"Picking up somebody who had fallen to the ground face-down is an abomination in this land," said Chief Wagbara. "Such person need not be picked up without sacrifices to the gods. By falling face-down, it means that they have either offended the gods or that they had done something abominable, which had contributed to their death."

"But Mrs. Harcourt had done nothing wrong," pleaded Mr. Nnadiekwe.

"You don't know that, do you?"

"No, I don't."

"Then?"

"So what can we do now?" asked Mr. Nnadiekwe anxiously.

"Nothing," replied Chief Wagbara, callously. "We cannot help you now. You have committed a crime yourself by picking her up. Therefore, we cannot help you. We must report back our findings to the Oha and the elders. Only they can tell us what to do."

"But she is dead, isn't she?" asked Mr. Nnadiekwe.

"That is what you said, didn't you," replied Chief Wagbara.

"Yes, then what do you say?"

"Nothing," said Chief Wagbara, "I didn't say anything; you said she is dead and we believe you. We did not come here to revive her; we do not have that power. We came here to ascertain the circumstances surrounding her death. You said she fell face-down and died. We are here to find out if that is the truth. And now you are telling us that you have picked her up, which means that you have tampered with the scene of the death and we can no longer ascertain the circumstances surrounding her death—a thing forbidden by the gods! Now we can no longer help you."

"I don't understand you," said Mr. Nnadiekwe.

"Well, you will soon find out," replied Chief Wagbara, as he and his men stormed out of the Waterside school and headed back to the palace of the Oha.

"What have you found?" questioned the Oha as soon as he saw Chief Wagbara and his men.

"Indeed, the woman is dead," replied Chief Wagbara. "But before we got there they had picked her up and laid her face-up in her bed."

"*Tuffia!*" spat the Oha in disgust. "Abomination! The unthinkable has happened in this land under my own watch and I am not happy! Go immediately and bring the White man and his men here. They must leave this land immediately before they bring calamity to all of us."

"About time!" shouted Chief Wagbara, as he and his men rose to return to the Waterside school. Meanwhile Reverend Harcourt had sent his messengers to the Church Mission Headquarters in Port Harcourt to inform the church officials and the British representative in Lagos about his misfortune, and preparation was underway for the transportation of his wife's coffin back to England, where she would be buried.

"The Oha and his council of elders want to see you immediately," said Mr. Nnadiekwe to Reverend Harcourt.

"What for?"

"I don't know."

"What do they want from me?" queried Reverend Harcourt. "They said they cannot help me because I picked up my dead wife from the ground. Now they are asking me to come and see them. What do they want from me now?"

"I don't know, sir."

"Well, let's go. Let me hear what they have to say." By the time Reverend Harcourt and Mr. Nnadiekwe arrived at the palace of the Oha, news that *Ohiomini* had lived up to his might and killed the wife of the White man had spread throughout the villages, and the villagers were pouring into the Waterside School to see and hear for themselves. Some hung out at the Oha palace after they learned that Reverend Harcourt was on his way there.

"They said you wanted to see me," said Reverend Harcourt to the Oha and his council of elders.

"Yes," replied Oha Achinike.

"What for?"

"Regarding what had happened to your wife."

"What about it? She is dead and I have accepted my loss."

"Yes, I see, and you should," said the Oha. "That is the way it is. The living must accept the death of the dead. No one is above death. All of us will die one day. I will die one day. Everyone here will die one day. And we must accept that fact or risk worrying ourselves to death!"

"Yes, you are right," said Reverend Harcourt. "But what did you call me for."

"Indeed," continued Oha Achinike. "I have called you here for a reason."

"And what is it?"

"The circumstances surrounding your wife's death."

"What about it?"

"You said she fell face-down and died, eh?"

"Yes, and—?"

"You cannot bury her on the soil of this land."

"I wasn't planning to," replied Reverend Harcourt. "But if I was, why not?"

"She had died an abominable death," replied Oha Achinike.

"What do you mean? What is so abominable about her death?"

"You said she died face-down."

"Yes, so what?"

"Well, such kind of death is an abomination in this land."

"What is the difference?" shouted Reverend Harcourt through his interpreter, Mr. Nnadiekwe. "Death is death. Why does it matter if someone died face-down as opposed to face-up?"

"The latter is normal, and the former is an abomination in this land," replied the Oha sternly.

"So what is the offence for dying abominably in your village," inquired Reverend Harcourt.

"It simply means you cannot bury her on the soil of this land."

"If not the soil ..., then where?"

"The Evil Forest."

"You mean if I had planned to bury my wife in this village, I would have to bury her in that filthy place?"

"Shut your mouth!" shouted Chief Wagbara. "*Ohiomini* is not filthy. *Ohiomini* is god. *Ohiomini* judges justly and fairly. *Ohiomini* does not offend whoever does not offend him. You have offended him and you have seen the might of his vengeance. Keep asking for his trouble and you will know that he is ruthless and fearless. Keep provoking him and you will feel the fire of his breathe!"

"Quiet!" the Oha said to Chief Wagbara, who was by now uncontrollable and deeply agitated beside himself. "Let him talk."

"I have nothing else to say," said Reverend Harcourt. "I cannot sit here and listen to your primitive nonsense. I believe in God, and I believe that it is God's will that my wife had died, not because of the power of any corpse-eating god!"

"Hush your mouth!" interjected Chief Wagbara, again.

"But do you believe that you have offended *Ohiomini* and that is why your wife had died?" asked Oha Achinike.

"No," replied Reverend Harcourt, "I have offended no one."

"Why not?"

"What offence have I committed?" asked Reverend Harcourt. "I saw two healthy children being wasted because they happened to be born twins and I intervened. Is that why my wife should die? I don't think so. That is not why she died. She died because her time had come and God wanted her for a reason. She did not die because your so-called *Ohiomini* killed her. I don't believe that. I will never believe that—not as long as I still believe in the power of the Almighty God! Go behind me, Satan!"

"Well, you had better believe it and from it learn," replied the Oha, somewhat irritably. "Otherwise you will pay more prices. And if you continue to be stubborn and incorrigible, we will ask you to leave our land!"

"Is that a threat?"

"No, an admonition," said Oha Achinike firmly.

"Well, it is not by your power that I am here," shouted Reverend Harcourt, "and it is not by your power that I will leave. I am here by the power vested in me by Her Majesty, the Queen of England, as well as in service of the Church of England, and it is by their authority that I do what I do. I will continue to do what they had asked me to do in this land until they recall me. I am not here to do any of your biddings but the bidding of Almighty God."

"And neither will we accept your rampage in this village like a 'born again' maniac!" bleared Chief Wagbara. "Continue on that path and you will see whose land this is!"

Chapter 7

A Dreadful Sight

The meeting between the Oha and his council of elders and the White missionary, Reverend Douglass Harcourt, ended with a bitter and a fierce exchange between the two parties. Reverend Harcourt did not appreciate the chief's suggestion that he, a White man, a devout Christian, and one who had no affiliation whatsoever with the so-called gods of the land, should offer an apology to an idol god to avoid its future wrath. He also did not appreciate his suggestion that had he intended to bury his wife in the village of Rumuachinva as opposed to transporting her body back to England, he would have to let them throw her into the so-called Evil Forest for animals to devour her body. "What a filthy gang!" he murmured to himself as he and Mr. Nnadiekwe were trekking back to the Waterside school.

Despite what had happened, the school remained open, and the assistants and the pupils went about their normal business in compliance with Reverend Harcourt's directives. Although some parents withheld their children from the school during this topsy-turvy period, Reverend Harcourt was sure that were the bulk of the pupils at his school the so-called hardworking children of the village, the "strong ones," as opposed to the "weak ones," their parents would have stopped them completely from attending school, for fear of the wrath of *Ohiomini*. But they were mostly the "weak ones" now, the ones nobody wanted, and so they could care less what happened to them. When he and Mr. Nnadiekwe returned to the school, they went into the classrooms to see that things were still under control. Then they returned to Reverend Harcourt's house. The messengers who had gone to Port Harcourt to inform the Baptist Mission and the colonial government officials there about the tragedy that had befallen Reverend Harcourt had not returned. They could do nothing than wait, since the messengers had also been instructed to make arrangements and return with them the casket that Mrs. Harcourt will be buried in.

As they waited patiently inside the house, they heard the scream of one of the pupils and they rushed out.

"What is it?" shouted Mr. Nnadiekwe.

"Look, look!" pointed the pupil.

"Oh, my God!" shouted Reverend Harcourt, who was walking beside Mr. Nnadiekwe. By now all the children and their teachers and assistants were out of their classrooms and curiously looking at what their classmates were pointing at."

"Wasn't that the same caskets we buried the twins?" asked Reverend Harcourt.

"Of course, they are," replied Mr. Nnadiekwe.

"Were they not buried six feet under?"

"I dug the ground myself," replied one of the assistants. "It was exactly four feet, or, perhaps, more."

"Then, why are they out of the ground and in the open?" asked Reverend Harcourt. "What sort place is this? What kind of land is this that won't even let the dead rest? They killed them and now they won't let them rest in peace? Why has the caskets risen to the surface? How can anyone explain this? Mr. Gabriel, go immediately and tell the Oha and his men to come and take them. I will have nothing else to do with them any longer!"

"Yes, sir," replied Mr. Nnadiekwe as he went off.

"What had happened again?" asked one of the chiefs as soon as he saw Mr. Nnadiekwe and his worried look. "Is something else the matter?"

"Yes! Yes!" replied Mr. Nnadiekwe. "Something else had happened, great father. Reverend Harcourt wants the Oha to send people to come immediately and see what had happened."

"What is it?"

"Just come and see for yourself," he pleaded. "I cannot explain it."

"What is it that you can't tell us, young man?"

"There is nothing to tell you; you have to see it to believe it," said Mr. Nnadiekwe. "I have heard that things like what you are about to see happens, but I had never actually witnessed it happen. Now that I have seen it I can't even believe my eyes. Please come and see it. I can't tell you; you will have to see it for yourself to believe it," ranted Mr. Nnadiekwe as he rushed back quickly to the Waterside school. And immediately, a group of men, including the chief priest of *Ohiomini*, Chief Uzor Wagbara trouped to the scene of the omen. They had barely entered the compound of the Waterside school when Chief Wagbara saw what he thought was why they were there—the twain caskets of the twins!

"*Arusi!*" he shouted, somewhat jubilantly. "I told you people you are playing with fire. This land does not eat what is impure. Give *Agbarauku* a filthy food and it will vomit it. Feed *Ohiomini* an impure meat and it will throw it up in your face. Look at that!" he wailed. "Just look at it," he pointed, "the woods are not even rotten. Even the maggots are afraid to eat what is not theirs, what belongs to the gods. It had been seven months since this incident took place and the gaskets are not even rotten, and I believe the bodies are as clean as it was when they were buried!" he lamented.

"Take them! Take them with you, you filthy scoundrels," shouted Reverend Harcourt. "I want no parts in your evil ways. Take them to your so-called Evil Forest. I have tried to do good for the twins, but I guess it doesn't pay to render help to you people. This is why you are backwards and will remain so for a long time."

"That is not what we have come here to do," replied Chief Wagbara. "We have not come here to be insulted in our own land, and we have not come to take the twins either."

"Then, what have you come to do?" asked Reverend Harcourt.

"We have come here to see. And now that we have seen, we will report back to the people who sent us."

"Then do so quickly and come and remove these things from my sight."

"But you are the one who brought them here."

"So?"

"So, you remove them yourself."

"I certainly will not."

"Then they will remain here for you," raved Chief Wagbara mockingly.

"That can't be," replied Reverend Harcourt. As they were haggling over what should happen to the gaskets, the envoy from Port Harcourt arrived. Among them were nurses, doctors, several police men and other important government and church officials. "Arrest them," Reverend Harcourt ordered the police. "Arrest those evil men. They claim to have caused my wife's death. And now they do not want to remove the coffins they had brought to my yard." The men tried to scramble away. Some succeeded, but others were not so lucky. They were overpowered, about seven of them, and handcuffed immediately while the frightened natives watched.

When news got to the Oha and his council of elders that Chief Uzor Wagbara, the chief priest of *Ohiomini* and six other men had been arrested by the police, anger swelled among them. They could not believe that the White man whom they had harbored among them could bring them such trouble. He had brought bad omen on himself by his act, and now he is tormenting the village and its people. The Oha and his council of elders sent more messengers to inform Reverend Harcourt about their rage and to summon him immediately before them. But before the messengers arrived at the Waterside school, the entourage and Reverend Harcourt had already departed for Port Harcourt. Accompanying them were

Mr. Nnadiekwe and two other assistants. The remaining assistants and the teachers were instructed to take care of the school until Reverend Harcourt and Mr. Nnadiekwe returns.

Meanwhile, the seven men had been un-cuffed and released under Reverend Harcourt's instruction, pending his return from England to bury his wife. Their only punishment in the meantime was to take the coffins of the twins back to the evil forest. But this was a tall order for the men to obey. Nothing of the sort had ever happened before in this village, and they did not know how *Ohiomini* would react to them. Instead they pleaded that Reverend Harcourt's assistants, most of whom were from neighboring or far, far villages to take the coffins back to the evil forest. But Reverend Harcourt would hear none of it. Either they do his bidding now or they would be taken to Port Harcourt and locked up in jail there until he returns from England. Given this option, the men had no choice but to take what they believed to be the less risky one. They accepted to take the corpses back to the forest themselves. However, shame and embarrassment would not let them do it in broad-daylight, so they protested that they would do it at night, which Reverend Harcourt opposed sternly.

"Take those filthy things out of my sight now," he fumed. "I never want to leave here thinking that those things are still in my compound. Just take them with you now!" he barked. With the help of the police and the government officials, the men were forced to obey the Reverend's orders immediately. But Chief Wagbara would hear none of it and instead offered himself to be handcuffed and taken to Port Harcourt than do the bid of the Reverend.

"It is against the law of this land," he protested.

"Do you prefer to go with us to Port Harcourt and be locked up there, or do you prefer go home to your wife?" asked one of the policemen.

"I don't care," responded Chief Wagbara. "All I know is that we cannot take the caskets to *Ohiomini* ourselves. It is unheard of." But the police would not let themselves haggle with a common villager. So they ordered that Chief Wagbara himself, not his helpers, to

The Victims of Rivalry

carry one of the casket and he did without hesitation, while a gun was being pointed at his head.

The men had barely turned the corner to go inside Achinva village when Reverend Harcourt and his entourage departed to Port Harcourt. The procession of Chief Wagbara and his men was a sight to see, and almost the entire village poured out to see them. Spectators poured in from every corner and, for a while, the village was in a state of pandemonium. As the men were about to turn the corner, heading towards *Ohiomini*, the procession came to a halt. The men carrying the coffins would not move. They merely spurned around and headed back into the village, this time running. They ran as fast as they could, with the coffins still in their heads. The villagers could not believe what they were witnessing, for such had never happened before. The now noisy crowd followed from behind them. Chief Wagbara and his men ran past the Church, past the Arena of the First Sons, and then headed to the palace of the Oha, where the Oha and his council of elders were eagerly awaiting their return. But instead they saw what everyone believed was the worst of abominations—the Chief Priest of *Ohiomini* carrying a casket of dead corpses! Oha Achinike could not believe his eyes, and neither could the people sitting with him.

When they saw the procession, they immediately stood up. Being one that communes with the gods and the ancestors, the Oha knew immediately what to do. He took out his staff and goatskin bag and horn and ordered the horn filled with wine. He then proceeded to meet the casket carriers on their track. He called on the gods and on the ancestors and made his supplications known to them. He promised them more sacrifices and appeasements, for a wrong had been done to the land. And that wrong was heavy and unforgiving and required special attention, lest the land of Achinva be cursed!

"We are witnessing an abomination," he said, and poured the wine on the ground. "This is unprecedented and unheard of. We do not know where this sort of thing came from, as we have never had prior experiences. Please," he pleaded with the gods and the ancestors, "tell us what to do. Otherwise, let these coffins go in peace to where they belong. *Agbarauku,* if we have wronged you it was not our fault. *Ohiomini,* if anyone has offended you, move swiftly and go after the perpetrator. We have done nothing to earn your disrespect. What had happened is most unfortunate, but we are not to blame. The White man asked for your wrath, *Agabrauku*—take your wrath to him and leave us alone, for we have done no wrong to you. If a child is not ashamed to die in broad-daylight, then why should the people taking him or her to the Evil Forest in broad-daylight be ashamed? Let the men return these coffins to you. Let them return them to where they belong, we beg you. We plead with you!"

After uttering these words and pouring his libations, the men carrying the coffins turned around and headed back to the *Ohiomini*. This time it was for real. They ran and never turned around or looked back, and they never stopped anywhere until they reached their final destination—the heart of *Ohiomini*. The men were exhausted and out of breath. And so instead of burying the corpses as was the tradition, they merely deposited them in the open air and fled the scary scene as swiftly as they entered it.

Chapter 8

The Exorcism of Evil

After Reverend Harcourt returned to England to bury his wife, another White man, Dr. Ronald Forester, was brought to temporarily take his place. Dr. Forester was not the amiable and friendly type. He looked mean and unlikable. The natives did not like his ways, and neither did the Churchgoers whom he presided over. But he didn't seem to care who liked or didn't like him, and this his non-caring attitude to everything made his relationship to the natives worse. As long as the pupils came to school to learn, and church wardens organized the church every Sunday for him to go in and preach, Dr. Forester had no other business with the village. Unlike Reverend Harcourt who had learned the ways of the native people and mingled with them at the direction and permission of the Oha and his council of elders in order to enable him recruit his school pupils, Dr. Forester had made no effort to mingle with the people. He didn't have to. After all, his predecessor had done everything for him. Not even once had he visited the Oha and his council of elders. And when they sent for him, he snubbed at them and refused to honor their invitation. Some people speculated that he was afraid that what had happened to Reverend Harcourt's wife would also happen to his own wife. Others surmised that he was feeling too superior and acting too educated for his own good.

"Who does he think he is, anyway?" some would murmur under their breath, whenever talks about him arose. But the man did not budge. He always kept to himself at his Waterside home, along with his wife and his assistants and cared less what the natives thought about him and how he carried himself.

Soon, however, a friction between him and his assistants, which had been fermenting for months, came to the fore. Mr. Gabriel Nnadiekwe, who was an elder in the church and was the supervisor of the school assistants and the number one interpreter of the school and the church, was abdicated and banished from both the church and the school. No detailed explanation was given as to why he was let go. Dr. Forester had in his place put someone else. But Mr. Nnadiekwe was a fighter, and would not go down without a fight. So the moment he received notice from Dr. Forester that he was no longer a part of the school and was not to step his feet on any of the church or school premises, he petitioned the Baptist Church Headquarters in England, bypassing the regional headquarters and head office in both Enugu and Port Harcourt, respectively. His petition seemed to have struck a chord among the church leaders in England. Six months later, or, perhaps, less than six months, Reverend Harcourt returned.

Reverend Harcourt's return was hailed as a victory of sort over "evil-Forester," as Dr. Donald Forester was later referred by the natives and the pupils at the Waterside school. But the six months Reverend Harcourt was away had changed him a lot, and he had come back a changed man. He was not the same jovial and compromising man that left. He looked more determined, and acted more like one on a mission. At the pulpit of the church, he preached as forcefully and as vehemently as he had never done before, and outside the church he spoke loudly and advised the villagers to turn from their evil ways and to totally banish idol worship and in its place put God Almighty.

"Who is this God Almighty you always talk about?" a villager, Elechi Emewhule and a group of men asked Reverend Harcourt one day, as he conversed with them during one of his regularly scheduled outings. "Is it not the same *Chineke* that we worship?"

Now, Elechi was known throughout Achinva village as a troublemaker. He was argumentative and a born skeptic. Indeed, a true son of the village. As far as anyone in Achinva could remember, Elechi had never left any case un-argued, and no one doubted that he was good at what he does, for his knowledge and common sense was broad and vast. He smiled easily, and it did not take much to make him laugh out loud. He was never angry. Although his eyebrows were bushy and his lips full, he was handsome in his stoutly built frame.

"Yes, He is the same as your *Chineke*," responded Reverend Harcourt to Elechi's question.

"Then why do you talk as if we do not know Him?"

"If you know Him, as you claim," responded Reverend Harcourt, "where do you worship Him?"

"What do you mean?" asked Elechi.

"I mean, before I came and built the Church house, where did this village worship the *Chineke* that you said you believe in?"

"Nowhere."

"Then why do you say you worship Him?"

"Do we have to build a house for Him to worship Him?"

"Not necessarily, but the scripture advises us to build a place of worship for the Lord."

"That is because you have a scripture that is giving you directions on what to do," quipped Elechi. "We do not have the luxury of a scripture, and we never had one. So we do not have the same direction that you have, and we believe that, perhaps, *Chineke* did not want us to have that direction. Perhaps it is neither important nor necessary to have that direction to know Him. Otherwise He would have given it to us. This is why we believe that the way we worship Him is just fine with Him."

"But how do you worship Him if you don't have a place to worship Him?"

"That is exactly my question to you," muttered Elechi. "Do we have to have a place to worship before we can worship him?"

"Why not?" replied Reverend Harcourt. "Do you not have a forest for evil, which I believe happens to be what you truly worship? Do you not have a house for *Agbarauku*, the so-called god of the land, which you claim to be the grand god that is protecting your land? Do you not have a shrine for *Osumini*, which you claim to be the god of the seas? And do you not have a shrine for *Amadioha*, which you claim to be the god of thunder and lightning?"

"Yes, you are right, we have all those things," replied Elechi.

"Now show me either a forest or a house or a shrine that you have built for the *Chineke*, who you claim to believe in, and whom you suppose to have created all things both in the heavens and here on earth?"

"No," said Elechi, "we have no forest, no house, and no shrine for *Chineke*. But that is our choice, and that choice is not without a reason."

"What reason could that possibly be?" asked Reverend Harcourt. "If you can build a house for other gods, why not one for *Chineke*, the one entity that you, rightly I might add, claim to have created all things, including the gods that you worship and have created forests for, built houses for, and devoted shrines to?"

"You know, Reverend Harcourt," said Elechi as he paused for a while, "I am glad you have observed this of our people. I have been meaning to have this discussion with you or anyone of you missionaries that have ministered to us about God Almighty. I tried to approach the other man who had just left, Dr. Forester, but he appeared lukewarm, so I left him alone. But you are different. You stir my brain by the way you talk and interact with us, and I believe that this entire village appreciates your presence and your ministry. When that tragedy struck in your home, we mourned for you bitterly and we prayed that you find it in your heart to come back. And we prayed that nothing happens to you again. In fact, this village was so touched by your loss that we never wanted anything to happen to your family again, even though we were afraid it could."

"Why?"

"Because *Ohiomini* never forgives easily until it is satisfied. It will continue to kill and pester whoever offends it. Because we feared for your life, we, the entire village, asked our Oha and his council of elders to offer sacrifice to appease *Ohiomini*, the Evil Forest. And they did. That is why we believe you are here and alive with us today!"

"Well, that is your belief," laughed Reverend Harcourt. "That is not my belief. I believe that the Almighty God protected me, and it was He who brought me back here."

"I don't mean to bring back memories or anything of that sort, Reverend, but if you are so sure that the Almighty God protected you, why didn't He protect your wife?"

"That I cannot answer," replied Reverend Harcourt. "I don't know about that claim. In fact, I honestly don't know. My wife may have died of fever or anything like that. I don't know. Nevertheless, I believe she died a natural death. I don't believe your god had anything to do with it."

"True, maybe," said Elechi. "But then you can also say that it is your faith that protected you."

"True, indeed—and always!"

"So it is your faith, not the house that you built for *Chineke* that protected you."

"Certainly!" said the Reverend.

"Now, as a Christian," continued Elechi, "do you necessarily have to be in a church house to be protected and looked after by the Almighty God?"

"Not necessarily."

"Indeed, you are right. I am glad you answered that way. And, believe it or not, that is what we in this village believe."

"What?"

"That knowing *Chineke* is simply having faith in him. And no more," said Elechi.

"What do you mean?" asked Reverend Harcourt.

"Well, let me explain," said Elechi. "We in this village believe that you do not necessarily have to build a house for him to know him. Knowing him, we believe, is accepting him totally and completely without questions asked. We also believe that no house can contain him, for he is too large and too mobile and too universal for a single, or even a multiple house, to contain him. He is everywhere, and his house is everywhere. So why would we want to limit him by building a house for him. The universe is his house. He built it. He created it. So why limit him in his own house. Why create compartments for him.

"If you think of it deeply," continued Elechi, "the only place we can truly build a house for him is in our hearts, which we carry everywhere we go, and even in death! We in this village understands this aspect of him completely. We in this village know him in our own way, and that is why you will never succeed in convincing anyone of us who knows and is aware of these things, such as myself and the Oha and his council of elders, and all the elderly men and women in this village, to abandon their trust and beliefs to come to your church on Sunday. But, again, why Sunday, of all day? Why not every day? After all *Chineke* is with us every day. And he protects us every day."

"I understand where you are coming from, but you have not answered my question," said Reverend Harcourt.

"Which is?"

"Why have you designated a forest for evil, built a house for *Agbarauku*, and built a shrine for *Osumin*i and *Amadioha* and none for *Chineke*."

"Well, Reverend Harcourt, those are minor gods," replied Elechi. "Those we can see and we can relate to because they are physical. We can touch them if we want to. We have, by the power vested in us by *Chineke* himself, kind of reduced them, by making them physical. And this was a deliberate act, I should add, perhaps so we can be able to touch them and even dine and commune with them. But *Chineke* is irreducible. He is untouchable. In fact, we believe that the gods are merely messengers of *Chineke*. We believe that they form a link between *Chineke* and us. But *Chineke* is too mighty, and too universal to be represented with either a statue or a forest or a shrine. He is everywhere and nowhere, within and without, and as such enigmatic and incomprehensible. And truly the only justice that can be done for such an incomprehensible entity, we believe, is the belief that He exists and that He is the judge of everything we do, and that He is in his throne judging all of us every day and will do so forever and ever!"

"Amen!" said Reverend Harcourt.

Chapter 9

A Legacy: The Twin Tale

Reverend Harcourt returned to his house at the Waterside school later that evening, after having had that lengthy conversation with Elechi Emewhule, whom he had previously considered a commoner among the natives, but an intelligent one nonetheless. What made him to strike up a conversation with this man and his friends, all of whom merely listened, he did not know. But now that he had, he was glad he did. Before now, however, he had had lengthy conversations regarding God and man and the gods of the village with men he considered prominent in the village, in an effort to convert them to Christianity so that they, in turn, could be his strong voice and agent in converting the rest of the recalcitrant village people. He saw the village of Rumuachinva as laden with evil due mainly to the people's strong belief in their gods and their ancestors. Now that he has had the unfortunate opportunity to experience what evil can do to the psyche of a people after it had gripped it from inside out, he now knew how much work he had to do to make the people believe in God first and then convert to Christianity next.

Before—that is before his wife died—he was merely scratching on the surface of this evil. But this common man, Elechi, through their conversation, had given him a new energy, a renewed vigor.

He had given him a reason to fight fire with fire. He was now determined to fight. The natives have a distorted view of God and what He is all about, he reasoned. The reason they do not come in droves to the church he had built for them was because they believe that there is God everywhere and, therefore, they need not build a house for Him. In a way, thought Reverend Harcourt, their reasoning made sense, for God is truly everywhere, but he was not going to accept their argument, reasonable and convincing as it may sound. He will insist, instead, that God, like all the other gods they had chosen to build a home for, needed a shrine—the church in this case—and that the shrine needed people to worship in it, in atonement and in acceptance of God as the Almighty. He will use their own argument against them and perhaps win some converts. Yet, he knew that it was going to be a daunting task, an uphill battle if you will, but one that he was willing to undertake, win or lose.

Meanwhile, before he had this conversation with Elechi, which was one day after he returned from England with two other visiting missionaries, Mr. Trent Williams and Dr. Timothy Cliffton, he had visited with the Oha and his council of elders and a few other prominent members of the village of Rumuachinva, who happened to be at the court of the Oha when he arrived. "Welcome back, Reverend Harcourt," Oha Achinike had greeted him that day the moment he saw him and two of his friends and his interpreter, Mr. Nnadiekwe. "Thank you, I am glad to be back," he remembers saying before their meeting began. It was a meeting that began earnestly but quickly turned serious—yet one that set a new tone for what was to shape his relationship with the village of Achinva and its inhabitants. The memory of this brief encounter still rings a bell in his head. And this was how it began:

"We are deeply sorry for your loss," said Oha Achinike, perhaps for the third time.

"So am I," replied Reverend Harcourt.

"I see you have new friends."

"Yes," he replied and took the liberty to introduce his friends. "This is Mr. Williams, and this is Dr. Clifftton. They are both from England and strong members of the church."

"Welcome, all of you to Rumuachinva," said Oha Achinike to the visitors. After the men had sat down, kola-nut and wine were served. Neither the men nor the Reverend ate or drank anything. They declined the offer politely, and he went straight to talk about why he and the men were there.

"Your Highness," said Reverend Harcourt, "we have come here for a reason. After what had happened, and before I sent my wife's body home, it was and still is my profound belief that your village needs our help."

"How do you mean? What type of help?" the Oha asked, as he leaned forward in his chair.

"Your village is full of evil, and your practices are too primitive for our church and our school to stay here and prosper. Some of your laws and customs will have to be changed or, perhaps, be modified. Otherwise we may have to relocate. I don't see how we can continue to stay here if we don't seem to be making progress."

"Do you mean to say that our culture and traditions are too primitive for you?"

"Yes, but I wouldn't put it so bluntly," replied the Reverend.

"And you think you can make amends somewhere. And as such you have come with your friends to civilize us or to make us less primitive?"

"No, we have come not to civilize you," the Reverend backtracked somewhat. "We have come to show you how to steer away from some of your evil practices."

"That is just what I said; you have come to civilize us."

"Well, if you put it that way, yes."

"Then say it, if that is what you mean, my friend," said Oha Achinike.

"Yes, that is exactly what I mean," replied the Reverend.

"Good, and now we can have a conversation. You see, my friend," said the Oha after clearing his throat and sipping some wine, "we

The Victims of Rivalry

in this village are a strong people. We know what we know and we don't know what we don't know. But that which we know, we take pride in knowing it. And that which we don't know, we make no claim to knowing. Why am I saying these things? I have often heard you, in this very hut, talk about civilization and how your church and your God will give us light and civilize us. Now, admittedly, I may be naïve to what you mean exactly, but I can, without equivocating, tell you that we in this village know exactly who we are. We are not standing on a quicksand here. We have a strong footing, we know where we are, and we know where we are going. I may not know the full definition of what you mean by civilization, but I can assure you that we have eyes and that we can see. And as far as we can see, we are a civilized people, irrespective of what your definition of that word might be."

"But, Your Highness . . .," interrupted Reverend Harcourt.

"Hold on . . ., you will have your say," assured Oha Achinike. "Let me first finish. Now, as I was saying, does that mean that we are a perfect people and that we have no room, here and there, for modification in our way of thinking and doing things? Of course, no! Only a blind in intellect will say and believe that. We are humans after all. We are not all perfect. We have human heads, human feelings, and human limitations. We know that the world is large. We are aware of the world out there, believe it or not. We may not have traveled it as you have, but we are aware that a world larger than ours exists. Indeed, simply put, we are not as naïve as we may seem.

"Now, you have traveled the world, you and your friends, I am sure," continued Oha Achinike, "and perhaps more than any of us here in this village can ever dream. If you know something that we don't know, tell us. If you know something that you believe is not right with our village, tell us what it is. As I said, we are not a perfect people, we have never claimed to be, and we will never claim to be as long as there is a *Chineke*, who knows and owns everything! Our life on this earth is temporary, and so are yours and that of your friends and your Queen in England. The only way we can live well on this earth and prosper is to learn from one another and from those who know more than we know, so that we do not live it completely by false pretenses. We do not like threats. We do not like to be threatened. And we do not associate with anyone who uses threat as a weapon for bargaining. When you first came to stay among us, you saw with your own eyes how agitated my people were. I don't think you can boast that they welcomed you with open arms. But with time, their hostility and lack of understanding subsided. I believe, also, that with time, we can get through anything, no matter how difficult and challenging.

"So, my friends, tell us the tale that your brain harbors," continued Oha Achinike. "What have you observed about our village that we the natives have not observed? Tell us, and we will change it if we have to. We are not a hardheaded people. We have, over the years, learned to learn from our mistakes and from the mistakes of others. So tell us what is on your mind; pour some oil into our ears, as our people would say!

"I must warn you, however," insisted the old man, "that the one who has been in the bush longer knows the bush more that the one just entering into it. So be careful how you thread this thick forest!"

"Thank you, Your Highness, for the opportunity," said Reverend Harcourt. "What I have come here to discuss with you is a very sensitive matter. I don't know how you and your people would take it, but I am going to say it anyway. I am going to say it because I know it is right and had better be said than not."

"Go right ahead, say what you feel," responded Oha Achinike calmly, "as long as it is not as threatening as your previous comments minutes ago."

"No, not at all," said Reverend Harcourt. "I am here to talk to you about your tradition regarding twin children and other religious practices that to me spell the word 'evil' in bold letters."

"I had anticipated that," said the Oha.

"Anticipated what?"

"That you wanted to talk about our custom pertaining to the *ijima*."

"You had?"

"Yes, my friend, go on."

"Well, that's all I have."

"You mean that's all you have to say?"

"Yes."

"And what about the *ijima* and our religious practices?"

"I want you to implement some changes regarding how you treat twin children in your village."

"What changes, my friend? Speak your mind."

"Well, first of all, why do you throw twin children into the Evil Forest?"

"To keep away evil!" replied the Oha.

"That is, of course, expected," smiled Reverend Harcourt. "Are you saying twin children are evil?"

"No, my friend, I am not saying that," replied the Oha, who was by now feeling somewhat uneasy. "You see, that practice has been going on in this village long before I was born. Our people believe that a woman is supposed to have only one child at a time. If she happens to have two or more than one, we say it is an abomination. And when things as abominable as that happen, we treat it the best way we know how. When an abominable thing happens, we treat it the way an abominable thing should be treated. In this case of twin children, which we know to be an evil omen, we throw the two children into the Evil Forest where we know they belong. If someone dies an abominable death, in other to ward off evil and to rid the living of further evil omen, we bury that person at the Evil Forest. That way we will not have to deal with it in the future."

"So you truly believe that twins are an abomination?" asked the Reverend.

"Not me, per se, but the people; it is our general belief."

"What about you as an individual, what do you think?"

"I have no personal thoughts regarding that; it is what the people think that matter most. Indeed, it is not about what I think."

"So if the people die, you die as well."

"Indeed ... how else can it be? I am the people and the people are me."

"Then who is leading who?"

"I am leading them, and they are leading me; we are both leading each other."

"But, as their leader, do you lead blindly or with reason."

"How can you ask a question like that?" bleared Oha Achinike angrily. "Of course I lead with reason. Any good leader, which, in the name of the gods and the ancestors, is what I believe I am, must lead with reason. Otherwise his leadership will make no sense to him or the led, and the gods and the ancestors will not approve of it and neither will they bless it."

"So you can make changes where you think changes are needed."

"Indeed.... As I told you when you first visited with us, we are an open-minded people. We do not close our minds to truth, for we know that the truth is as loud as a gun-shot. And whenever it is spoken, truth that is, it is often loud and clear. We in this village do not muffle truth."

"Well," declared Reverend Harcourt, "I hope it does not baffle you that we, the church, believe that you and your people are wrong about the twins," declared Reverend Harcourt.

"Okay," replied Oha Achinike, shaking his head in agreement. "Why do you say that?"

"I say that to inform you that twins are not evil," continued Reverend Harcourt. "They are instead a blessing from God. Your gods may think that they are evil, but my God, whom your people refer to as *Chineke*, thinks that twins are a blessing to any family, and the womb that bore them is a blessing as well. Therefore, I am pleading that their lives be spared from henceforward. They are not the children of evil; they are the children of God."

"You know," said Oha Achinike after a long pause, "I have often thought so in my mind, but had never had the courage to point it out to my people. Ever since I was a child, I had puzzled over this tradition of ours. Why, I remember thinking at one time, do we accept twin yam tubers, twin cassava tubers, twin oranges, twin plantains, and twin everything else and we do not accept twin children. Instead we consider them an abomination and throw them away, alive, into the Evil Forest. I think you are right, my friend. We need to review that aspect of our tradition. I will have to talk with my people about it. I will get back to you once we reach a decision."

"And when will that be?" inquired Reverend Harcourt.

"Perhaps, tonight; isn't it amazing how sometimes minds think alike?" asked the Oha.

"It is true, indeed. And I want to see how far you will go with this very issue before I tell you all the other observations that I have made about your village."

"I will see to it," replied Oha Achinike.

That evening, probably six or so hours after Reverend Harcourt made his observation public, Oha Achinike sent the town crier to summon the villagers to the Arena of the First Sons early the next morning. When Reverend Harcourt heard the metal gong of the town crier and heard the interpretation of what he had to say from Mr. Nnadiekwe, he was thrilled. The villagers did not know what to make of such an impromptu summoning, especially since it was asking them to forsake their essential early morning trek to their farms. Some speculated that the White man and his people had come to demand reparation for the death of Mrs. Harcourt from the village. Others speculated that Oha Achinike and his council of elders had, perhaps, decided to force them to send their strong children to the White man's school and they were going to fight such order until death knocks on their ears.

So, in droves, and in groups of two and three, five and six, they gathered at the arena. The noise they made was deafening, for it was like a market place. You could not hear the one standing next to you unless you listened closely and quite literally lent them your ears. Such was the atmosphere when Oha Achinike and his council of elders entered the Arena of the First Sons. Immediately silence deafened the crowd. Not even a cough could be heard. As usual, they were attentive and eager to hear what their Oha had to say. "Achinva, *Anu meka!*"

"*Dee eli!*"

"Rumuachinva, *meka!*"

"*Dee eli!*"

"Achinva *meka!*"

"*Dee eli!*"

"Achinva *meka!*

"*Dee eli!*" roared the crowd.

"When the Oha greets his people four times, his brave people returns his greetings four times," said Oha Achinike. "You have done well to come at such short notice and in droves. I am happy to have a people who can respond to my call quickly, even though it was within a short notice. I thank all of you for coming. I know that many of you are by now speculating on why I have summoned you."

"Yes," roared the crowd.

"And you think you know why I have called you."

"Yes."

"Well, you don't," he said and the crowd roared, again, with laughter.

"I have called you so we can have a conversation," he continued. "What I am about to tell you now is a matter very important to me personally and one that I have thought about for a long time. As you all know, we are a peaceful people, and we are also an open-minded people. We take nothing for granted, and we do not want or like anything or anyone to take us for granted. When we make a decision about anything, we want that decision to be ours. We want to own that decision, and we want it to come from our hearts. We do not like to be coerced into making any decision that we know, for sure, does not favor us. That would be a death sentence, and we do not wish to die—not in our own hands, and certainly not in the hands of a foreigner to this land.

"Speaking of foreigners, I want each of you to send your condolences to Reverend Harcourt, our visitor, if you have not already done so. He is a good man, unlike his friend who had just departed. That man is a good man. He has a good heart. He has dealt with us with open mind and we appreciate him for that. As our people use to say: You only have to compare the apple you grow in your land with that grown in another man's land to know that yours tastes better. Otherwise you don't know. We have had the opportunity to compare one White man to another and have discovered that they, like us, are not uniform. They have differences in them, just as we do. There are bad ones among them, just as there are bad ones amongst us. Dr. Forester is bad. But Reverend Harcourt has proven to be good. And we like him. I am sure every one of you can avouch for that.

"When we told him that we cannot send all our children to his school," continued Oha Achinike, "he did not argue with us. He simply accepted our position. Now, that, my people, is what a visitor to a foreign land ought to do—accept what he or she cannot help or change, and he did exactly that. When he went back to his homeland to bury his wife, we, at least myself, thought he would never come back. But lucky for us, he came back. He had come back to continue to preside over his school and his church in our village. Those of you who find it in your hearts to attend his church, do so, and those who wish to send their children to his school, continue to do so. We don't know what tomorrow might bring; therefore, we must content ourselves with what today has brought to us, good or bad.

"But unlike his replacement, Dr. Forester, Reverend Harcourt is a good man. He has shown us his good side, and I believe there are much more that we can learn from him, unlike Dr. Forester who wore hate on his sleeves. One wonders why he even bordered to come among a people to whom he harbors so much hatred for. When you let a person who hates you teach you, he or she will teach you nothing but hate—how to hate yourself and how to hate other people. Such a person will teach you nothing that will make you better in life. Such a person will have nothing to teach us or our children. That is why we are happy that Reverend Harcourt has returned to us.

"Now, on the matter at hand, our friend, Reverend Harcourt, the White man, came to my palace yesterday," continued Oha Achinike after a moment of silence, "just one day after he returned from burying his diseased wife. He came to discuss something he had observed to be wrong, as he puts it, with our village—something that he believes we need to correct if we are to join the rest of the civilized world, which he had been to and none of us has ever been, him having traveled far and wide. But just as we found out that cassava can be eaten without upsetting the stomach, so can we one day find out whether he is telling us the truth or lying to us about his travels and his knowledge of the world beyond ours. Let us approach his suggestions with open-mind as we've always done with things that are not normally considered an aspect of our culture and tradition. After all, as the saying goes, nothing ventured, nothing had, and no steps taken, no inches gained!

"We all know what happened to Reverend Harcourt and his wife. I will not repeat the story. That was a situation neither of us could have averted. And I also know that some of you feel and believe that we must do something about what led up to that situation. I am talking about our treatment of *ijima* (twin) births. As I had indicated to some of you during private conversations, I happen to be one leaning in the direction of mercy. We must do something about our tradition regarding how we deal with twin children. I was a victim of that tragedy not long ago, as you all know. My youngest wife gave birth to twins and I watched them being taken alive to *Ohiomini*. To tell you the truth, I was not a happy man. But it is our tradition, and I had to comply with it, even though it was a hard decision for me to make and accept. Many of you went through the same thing. Well, we have come to the crossroads again, and I believe that it is time we did something about it." By now some people had began feeling restless. They wanted to speak, but the Oha would not give them audience. At least, not yet! He wanted to finish his thoughts first before letting agitators and descanters feast on his proposition. As such he continued non-stop.

"Yesterday," he continued, amid uproar and noise, "Reverend Harcourt came to my palace with his newly arrived friends. We had a lengthy conversation. During our conversation he revealed one thing I had always thought about regarding twin children and how we treat them. He told me that they were a special pair, and that they were a special gift from God—his God, which we refer to as *Chineke*. Well, my people, I began to reason with him on that issue, and after consulting with my council of elders and some of our elderly mothers and fathers who were at my palace yesterday when the White men visited me, we come to the conclusion that we must stop this practice."

After he said these last words, there were murmurs from the crowd, and it was undoubtedly one of disapproval. "Hear me out first, my people. You will have your say when your turn comes. But, for now, hear me out. Let me die before you bury me is what I have heard great speakers say."

"Go on, great father," shouted someone from the crowd.

"*Meka*," replied Oha Achinike. "From today onwards, I am proposing that we stop our practice of throwing our twin children into *Ohiomini*. I and a host of others happen to agree with the White man that twins are the children of God, not of evil as we had previously believed. We must change this tradition and we will appeal to *Ohiomini* to heed our plea to rescind this aspect of our tradition. Think about it. This tradition has been around even long before any of us was born. Perhaps something happened long ago that prompted our ancestors to take such a harsh stance against twin children. But nothing that we know of has happened of late to warrant us to hold on so strongly to this tradition, especially since it involves the taking of lives! I think we should break its back. Now!"

"Because the White man said so?" shouted someone in the crowd.

"No, not at all," shouted back Oha Achinike.

"Then why are we doing it now? Why didn't we do it before he complained?" shouted the same voice.

"That is a good question," echoed Oha Achinike. "But, quite frankly, the White man's complaints have nothing to do with our decision. If we had not considered that it was the right thing to do, he could have complained all he wanted and our position will never change. Indeed, and I want you to quote me on this: it does not mean that if the White man does not approve, the Black man does not improve. Put that notion out of your head, all of you! We have our own heads to think; and we have our own mind to make up."

"But that is what it seems like to me," shouted the same voice.

"No," replied Oha Achinike, "that is far from the truth. I had thought about this issue for quite some time now. It is true, however, that I had not taken the initiative until now. So, in a way, it would look like I had come forward with the plan because the White man complained. Yet, it is our tradition, and we have the final say. If we, the people, refuse to change it, it will not be changed. The White man is not going to put a knife on our throats if we do not do anything about it. He does not tell us what to do. Yet, I believe that he had done well by coming forward with his complaints. He does not want what happened to his wife to happen to someone else. And I think that is a legitimate reason for anyone to complain.

"Imagine for a minute. We accept twin cocoyam. We accept twin yams. And we accept twin fish, and twin antelopes. We eat these things without complaining that they are twins and we never died from eating them. We even offer goats that were born twins to our gods and they eat it without complaints, so why would we not accept the fact that children, too, can be born twins. I think that is just plain foolishness." Again, some in the crowd roared with disapproval.

"Twins are evil and the White man is evil," someone in the crowd shouted. "And we should get rid of them both."

"Twins are an abomination; if my wife bears them I will personally take them to the evil forest myself," shouted another. The Oha concluded his speech by asking the people to go home and think about his proposal. Those who still objected and have something to add to what he had said can come personally to him and his council of elders to lodge their complaints.

But the argument did not die there; it went on for a while without the villagers unanimously accepting the proposal of the Oha and his council of elders, along with some elderly mothers and fathers of Achinva. But a final decision was made for those who were still not convinced. These vigilantes and borderline advocates of a conservative past, as they were referred to by some villagers, wowed to take the law into their own hands and kill or take to the forest, alive, any twin whom the White man saves or rescues. Leading in this protest was Chief Uzor Wagbara, the chief priest of *Ohiomini*. Despite their protests, however, the Oha and his council of elders reached a final decision on the matter. Their decision was eventually accepted, but not unanimously still. In addition, they agreed to hand every twin children born in the village to the White man to train and educate in his school and in his church.

As circumstances would have it, just a fortnight after the entire village had had this conversation Egbeke, the wife of Weneka Ohavueze, the best friend of Elechi Emewhule, gave birth to beautiful, twin baby boys. But the boys were not properly welcomed, not as the tradition prescribed for welcoming new births, as neither parents nor their relatives were thrilled to have them.

Chapter 10

A Twin Journey

Just hours after the twins were born, the news of their birth spread throughout Rumuachinva village. It was the first twin birth since the long and arduous conversation the village had had with their leaders over the White man's objection to their age-old practice of casting away twins to the infamous Evil Forest, and so no one knew exactly what would happen to the twin boys. No one among the villagers doubted, however, that an omen had happened as a result of their birth. It was a matter of what to do with them. But the decision was beyond the mother and father and their immediate families. The decision on whether to keep the twins as the white man had advised or to cast them away as the tradition prescribed now rested in the hands of the Oha and his council of elders, who, in fact, had already made their decision. Only the parents and the immediate families of the twin were indecisive and as such were the ones still haggling over what to do with the children.

But while the fate of their twin boys were been decided by the elders, Egbeke and her husband were infighting as well. She desperately wanted to keep her two boys, whom she had suffered for nine months to carry in her stomach. But her husband, Weneka Ohavueze, and few others in his own side of the family, who still believed in the old tradition would have none of it. He did not

The Victims of Rivalry

want his name to be attached to such an omen. He did not want to be made an example or, as he put it, "be the first to alter a long tradition of the land!"

"It is enough, as they say in this village," he argued, "that a man whose sperm produced two eggs in a woman is cursed; it is even worse if anyone should keep the product of that pregnancy, which is considered an anomaly, an omen! I would not be part of it," he argued to his wife, "and if you, Egbeke, want to keep those twins, you will not do it in my house."

"Why are you quarreling with me as though I had done something wrong; as if I have the last say?"

"You are right, you don't; but you are acting as though you do."

"How?"

"By your actions."

"What actions, Weneka?" asked Egbeke. "Are you out of your mind? These are our children, are they not?"

"Yes, they are," replied Weneka. "But they are also an abomination in this land and I want no parts of them. If they didn't want to be treated this way, then they should have opted to be born like normal children. But this is what they want; this is how they want it. This is how they wish to disgrace me. But I will not let them. I will disgrace them before I let them disgrace me."

"How can you say that to your own blood?"

"No, they are not my blood; they are my bad blood."

"And mine, too, remember?" cried Egbeke. "They are ours and I have a say as to whether they live or die. I carried them for nine months. I suffered and labored over these children. Now you don't want them anymore. Well, too bad, I do."

"When did I say I don't want them?" blared Weneka. "Are you insane? When did I ever say I don't want them? Is it me or is it the tradition of our village that don't want them?"

"But are you not helping the tradition by objecting to their living?"

"How? How am I objecting to their living?"

"By supporting the agents of evil. At least, they have a chance now."

"What chance? What chance are you talking about, Egbeke? So you are calling our tradition an agent of evil? I hope you repeat what you just said in public and see what would happen to you."

"Watch me, I will say it and nothing will happen to me," shouted Egbeke.

"Go right ahead, say what you wish" said Weneka, as he was storming out of the house. "I told you I don't want to be part of it and that is that." But his leaving the house to get away from quarreling with his wife was short. He was too ashamed to venture into the village, for fear of what people might say to him. And so sooner than he left, he returned and sat down on the ground right in front of his house, distrust beyond explanation.

Minutes after he sat down, a group of men with machetes accosted him, entered his house, and forcefully snatched the twins from the grip of their grandmother, who was weeping incessantly for the hapless boys. The men then wrapped the twins up in a blanket and rushed out of the house. They moved swiftly and to the direction of the Evil Forest, cursing and intimidating anyone who tried to stop them. As the children wailed, their mother and relatives' anger flared with rage. Everyone inside the house, including Egbeke, speculated that Weneka had made the arrangement for the twins to be taken, as he merely stood by, speechless, and watched his own children being wrestled out of their grandmother's grip.

"I have had no hand in such a thing," said Weneka in bewilderment, as the accusation and finger-pointing grew. But no one would believe him. He cried and fell to the ground, shouting and avouching his innocence. Yet the mourners looked at him in disgust, and his agony could not be hidden.

"Then go after them and return the boys," one of the women shouted.

"I would do no such thing either," shouted Weneka.

"What seems to agonize you so much, my friend," said a voice to Weneka from behind him. "Why do you cry like a woman in labor?" When Weneka looked up, he saw Reverend Harcourt and Mr. Nnadiekwe.

"Oh, pastor, welcome to my house.... I'm a sad man. I'm hurting deep inside of me. Help me. Please, help me, pastor, help me."

"What seems to be the problem?"

"Yes, pastor ... my children! My children! Help them!"

"Don't mention it ... we already know," said Reverend Harcourt.

"You already know what?" asked Weneka, surprised.

"We already know about what you are agonizing about. And that is why we are here."

"Why?"

"To take the children."

"You are here to take the children? But they are no longer here," said Weneka under his deep sob. "They are already taken."

"What are you saying?"

"Oh, I thought you knew already."

"Knew what?"

"Oh, a group of men came here few minutes ago and took the children."

"When?"

"Few minutes ago."

"What did they say to you? Who sent them? And where did they take them?"

"They said that the Oha and his council of elders have objected to your plea and have instructed them to pick up the twins and take them to *Ohiomini*."

"But we are just coming from our meeting with the Oha and his council of elders. We had just convinced them that we will raise the twins in our church and in our school and they had accepted our offer. That is why we are here. We are here to pick up the twins."

"Then who are those men that were here not long ago?"

"We don't know. Perhaps some people have decided to take matters into their own hands."

"Do you know who they are?"

"Yes."

"And you didn't stop them?"

"No, I didn't. How can I—?"

"Why not?"

"Well, I thought the Oha had sent them."

"But the matter had long been decided. Were you not at the meetings, at the gathering, where it was decided that the children be raised in the church and at the school?"

"I don't know pastor—I just don't know—," cried Weneka, as he shook his head.

"Then let's go after them." Without revealing what had just transpired to Egbeke and the relatives inside the house who were still crying over the presumed loss, the three men rushed out and headed in the direction of *Ohiomini*, where they knew the men had taken the twins.

"I hope they don't kill them before we catch up with them," said Reverend Harcourt.

"No, they won't," said Weneka.

"Why are you so sure?"

"Because it is against our tradition to kill them before delivering them to *Ohiomini*. Especially if they are not already dead. Besides, it is believed that *Ohiomini* prefers them to arrive alive!"

"So chances are that they might still be alive."

"No doubt, they might still be alive" said Weneka. And just as he uttered these words, and after about a half mile of running in the narrow roads that led to the forest, they saw a group of men with machetes heading home from the Evil Forest. But the men did not see them. In order to avoid confrontation, they hid themselves in the bush, wasting just enough time to let the men pass. Once the men passed, the three men continued onto the interior of the Evil Forest. It was an unpleasant journey. Night was coming fast, and the path leading to the Evil Forest had fear ridden all over it. No one trod that path without wearing fear all over, and no one who had traveled its length would doubt that the spirits, both good and evil, were present and alive.

But the men did not care. They conversed among themselves and spoke out loudly in other to alley fear. They had with them a Bible, a lit candle, a torch light, and an incense—things that would naturally deter evil. The path was narrow, and so they could not walk side by side. They had to go in a single file, but no one wanted to be either first or last in the line, except, of course, Reverend Harcourt, who did not care where the two fearful men, whom he later dubbed unbelievers, put him. They put him first.

"Have faith, gentlemen," he said as he led the troupe. "We are doing nothing evil here. We are doing the work of God, and He will see to it that we complete it without any mishap."

Meanwhile news had spread in the village that vigilantes have taken matters into their own hands and taken the Ohavueze twins to the Evil Forest. It was the perpetrators themselves who boasted about what they had done that helped the news spread as fast as it did. The Oha and his council of elders were beside themselves. They fumed with rage over it and quickly summoned the warriors of the village of Achinva to go immediately to the Evil Forest and retrieve the children, a thing that was unheard of.

"Dead or alive, return the children," ordered the Oha. "Bring them here to me," he barked. "When the people take matters into their own hands and do as they wish without the guidance of the law of the land, it means that the corridors of governance has eroded. And I will have none of that. No! Not under my watch," he fumed. "Whoever was responsible for this will be punished severely."

The village warriors had barely lined themselves into the narrow path leading to the Evil Forest when they heard the cry of children. At first they did not know what to make of it, as it headed their way. However, one among them suggested that they hide in the bushes and from there observe what was amiss. Having not much time to haggle, they accepted the suggestion and hid themselves in the bushes. As they watched, they were surprised to see Reverend Harcourt, the White man, and Mr. Nnadiekwe, and Weneka, the father of the twins. But instead of stepping out of their hidings, they decided to trail them, as stepping out immediately would send a chilling fear to the spines of the Good Samaritans and cause them to panic needlessly.

Reverend Harcourt carried both children on his hands as the procession headed straight to the Church building, where multitudes of worshippers were now gathered, including Egbeke and her relatives, all of whom were in awe. Upon entering the church, the three men, along with the multitude of worshippers, knelt down near the altar and Reverend Harcourt began to pray loudly. He condemned the practice of throwing God's children away, and affirmed that twins were a blessing to a family, not a curse. And, henceforth, any woman who bears twins should bring them to the church to nurse and raise them for God! At the blessing of their mother, Egbeke, and their father, Weneka, he named the twins Israel and Saturday. He took them to his house afterwards, to raise and to educate them, and the names which he gave them that night remained their names to this day!

Chapter 11

Tradition and Trans-value!

Long after the twins incident occurred, and he was able, once again, to take fish of the sharks mouth, as the two incidents were being likened by the villagers, Reverend Harcourt and his brothers and sisters in Christ were emboldened to preach the gospel of Jesus Christ to the people by instructing them openly to avert from their old ways of acknowledging the non-existent powers of the devil above the Almighty, visible and practical powers of God. This new and bashful approach did not augur well with a lot of people in the village of Achinva, especially people who could not identify with the new religion, as well as people who had long ago made up their mind not to. These people had vested interest in the old, animist religion and were not willing to be swayed by the White man or his native converts and followers, no matter what, into accepting a foreign religion. These were the priests of *Ohiomini, Amadioha, Osumini, Agbarauku*,—and, indeed, more than half of the population of Rumuachinva village.

"It is not enough to believe that God or *Chineke* is Almighty," said Reverend Harcourt one day as he preached to Elechi Emewhule and his friends, whom he had conversed with previously and for the third time and had almost considered converts, "you also must believe in his son, Jesus Christ (who died so all of us can be saved) as your savior, as well."

It was a conversation that began earnestly, and, as usual, Elechi was the lone speaker, while his friends, who, perhaps, seemed intimidated to speak to a White man, merely listened. And whenever Elechi made a smart comment or asked a mocking or provoking question, which they expected he would ask, they laughed and patted him in the back, and did the same to one another in excitment. And so when Reverend Harcourt made the comment about Jesus being the son of God, Elechi's friends knew what was coming.

"Say it again, Pastor," said Elechi. "Who do you say died so all of us can be saved?"

"Jesus Christ, the son of God," repeated Reverend Harcourt in his usual eloquent manner.

"Chineke *mee!*" said Elechi in alarm. "I don't know if I am hearing you correctly, Pastor. Please make it clearer to me. Or I must be going deaf. Did you just say that your God—the *Chineke-*God we revere—have a son?"

"Yes!"

"You mean *Chineke*—the one who created the Heavens and the Earth—have a son?"

"Yes, indeed, my friend!"

"Really, a son, eh!" wailed Elechi. "We in this village didn't know that. Do any of you know that before?" he asked his friends.

"No," they replied unanimously.

"Well, my friend, there are many things about the Almighty powers of God that you don't know," boasted Reverend Harcourt.

"I think you are right, Pastor," said Elechi. "Yes, indeed, you are right. There are many things we in this village don't know about *Chineke*. And this is one of them. You said the name of that his son is Jesus Christ?"

"Yes, indeed," replied Reverend Harcourt.

"And he is the son of *Chineke.*"

"Yes, my friend."

"I don't think a lot of people in this village know what you are telling us now."

"No, they don't, just like you didn't know, except of course the people that come to church or read the Bible. And that is why I am here."

"Why?" asked Elechi.

"To share the good news with you."

"That is interesting, Pastor," said Elechi. "This is, indeed, mighty good news that more people in this village should hear and learn something from."

"Why? What makes it so interesting to you? And what do you suppose they would learn from it," asked Reverend Harcourt who had suddenly begun to sense a bit of cynicism in Elechi's comments.

"Why didn't we know this before, Pastor?"

"What do you mean?"

"Well, it seems to me that we in this village are the only people in the world who didn't know that *Chineke*-God has a son."

"Well, that is why I am here, I told you."

"Why?"

"To inform you, to educate you and your people on these kinds of things."

"Good of you, Pastor," said Elechi. "It is very good of you. So, pastor, if I may ask, I suppose your God also have a wife."

"Don't be silly!" roared Reverend Harcourt, somewhat angrily. "That is a ridiculous suggestion!"

"No, pastor, I am not suggesting anything," retorted Elechi. "You said He has a son. But you never mentioned his wife. So I reasoned that no one can have a son without having a wife. Or can they? Can anyone have a son and not have a wife? Does it happen in your country? Such things are not known to happen here, and it has never happened in our village. And I'm just wondering...."

"No, you are right my friend. Pardon my outburst. No one can have a child without a wife. And God did not have a wife."

"Then how did He get the son?"

"No, my friend, you are getting it all wrong," replied Reverend Harcourt calmly. "It seems that you have forgotten the Almighty powers of God."

"No, I have not," replied Elechi. "I just didn't know that His powers included having a child without having a wife. I have never seen that happen, never heard it before, and I have nothing to relate it to. Perhaps you have, in your country, and that is why you can relate to it and believe that it is possible as well."

"On the contrary," replied Reverend Harcourt. "I have not seen it happen either, not in my country and not anywhere."

"Then tell me, pastor, how *Chineke*-God could have had a son without a wife."

"Well, if you must hear it from me, Jesus was given birth to by a virgin—the Virgin Mary!"

"And did God live here on this earth with this Virgin Mary?"

"Live? Don't be ridiculous, my friend," frowned the Reverend. "Not at all, no! No, God did not live with the Virgin Mary on this earth."

"Then how did he impregnate her."

"Who said anything about impregnating her?"

"It seems, my friend, that you have forgotten or don't know who God truly is. If I can remember clearly, last time we spoke you gave me the impression that you truly know the Almighty powers of God, who you and your people call *Chineke*. Now I doubt that you knew what you were talking about. I doubt that you know him at all. Then, in that case, let me remind you: He is Almighty, All-knowing, and Everywhere! He is capable of any and everything. The world is His own and the universe is His own as well. He controls it. And He tells it and the people living in it what to do."

"But I know all that, pastor. I know about all His powers. And that is why we in this village accept him with all our heart and above all the other gods."

"And you also know that He is capable of anything?"

"Yes, but . . . including impregnating a virgin here on earth?"

"Now, that is blasphemy!" roared Reverend Harcourt. "I think you are overstepping the realms of our conversation."

"What is blasphemy?" asked Elechi.

"Blasphemy is saying what you just said about God," replied Reverend Harcourt.

"Which is?"

"I would dare not repeat what you just said; I am not foolish."

"And neither am I," replied Elechi, somewhat surprised by the Reverend's reaction to what he said. "But you started it, you know, pastor! How can you say that *Chineke*, whom we in this village and all the abounding clans and villages know to be almighty and all-knowing and who created all things great and small, and whom we respect above anything on this earth and beyond words, impregnated a virgin and had a son here on earth? How can you say something like that and not expect us, and especially me, to question it? You must take us for fools, which we are certainly not!"

"But that is not what I said," retracted Reverend Harcourt, intending to clarify himself. "That is what the scripture says. The scriptures are the words of God. I am merely an interpreter of the scriptures, and I am interpreting it for you and your people. I wish you could read it for yourself and you won't have to question me."

"I wish so, too, pastor," said Elechi excitedly. "I really wish I could read it for myself. But I am illiterate in your alphabets and letters. However, I know myself. And I know where I come from. And I know what questions to ask if I needed a direction. As such, I am not completely, in the layman use of the word, an illiterate. No. Not as long as I have a mouth and can speak with it. Now that reminds me . . . if I may ask, pastor, who wrote the scriptures?"

"The scribes and the Apostles."

"Who are these people?"

"Human beings like you and me who lived long ago."

"How did they write the scriptures? And how can the scriptures be God's words if human beings like you and me wrote them?"

"Well, from what I know, God either inspired or dictated it to them."

"In what language?"

"How will I know? That is a question you should ask God, not me. And I am sure that if you ask honestly, you also will get an answer honestly."

"You see, Reverend Harcourt," said Elechi, somewhat emboldened, "you strike me as an intelligent man and I respect you for that. In fact, I respect your people and all your accomplishments on this earth. But when you make an unintelligent comment like the one you made few minutes ago about *Chineke* having a son with a virgin, I begin to wonder about you and your religion. I don't know if you understand, but that is too huge a claim to make and expect no one to question from whence it came. By your comments, you must know that you have reduced *Chineke*, don't you? You have inadvertently, perhaps, reduced Him to the level of you and me, which he is not. He is now our equal, according to you, and that, to me, is the highest form of blasphemy! In a way, you have made Him seem as though He is one of us and susceptible to all the frailties of human beings, including the laughable impregnation of a virgin!—which is both amusing and, at worst, a foolish thing to say, for I have never heard of a pregnant virgin! Let alone a virgin Mother! These things trouble me, and I find them repulsive. Even offensive! You are insulting our intelligence!

"Now, you showed me the Bible and the scriptures, which you claim to have been dictated by God to human beings like you and me. As much as I doubt that claim seriously, I wonder why *Chineke* did not make such scriptures available to us here in Africa. Did He not find us worthy of their contents, or did He not detect among us here in Africa good scribes and Apostles? Or, maybe, He was trying to spare us some lies and distractions from holding on to our beliefs and strong faith in Him in our own little way. Who knows?

"I say these things for a reason, Pastor," continued Elechi. "And that reason is that, perhaps, your presence among us will shake off that strong belief that many of our people have in Him. Because of the things you are saying about *Chineke*, those who did not have reasons to doubt His almighty powers may now have a reason to do so. And you are to blame, unfortunately. Am I making sense to you at all? You just sit there and listen to me talk. You are not saying a word. Have I offended you?"

"No, my friend," muttered Reverend Harcourt, finally, and after a long, silent look that spelt disgust and bewilderment. "No, you are not making any sense at all. I kept silent because I was told by one wise man that 'silence is the best answer to a fool'."

"So I am a fool."

"Indeed, you are."

"Because I am not buying into your lies? Because I am not sitting here and saying yes, sir! yes, sir! to your hypocrisy!" blared Elechi.

"You see, Elechi," said Reverend Harcourt, smiling, "were I not a man of God, I would have cursed you to your face after hearing all you had to say."

"But you called me foolish; isn't that insulting enough?"

"Which, indeed, is what you are for saying all those things you said!"

"And so are you, Pastor," said Elechi angrily. "You are foolish to leave your country and come here to tell us bunch of lies and think none of us is intelligent enough to question the validity of what you preach. Go ahead, preach to the naïve, the foolish, the sheepish!—not to ones like me, for I know what you know and, perhaps, more, and you know nothing than lies and hypocrisy!"

"I am disappointed in you, Mr. Elechi; in fact, I regret stopping to converse with you," said Reverend Harcourt to the man whom he had almost considered a friend and a true convert. "You were such a nice person when we spoke last time and you spoke so well, even though you objected to some things I said. What has come over you, Mr. Elechi? I found you, then, intelligent and worthy of my company. But now I have a different opinion of you. I think you are both a poison and a disgrace to the people of this innocent and peace-loving community, and you should be ashamed of yourself!"

"Why?" asked Elechi. "Because I am not primitive enough for you? Or, because I am not letting you civilize my already civilized mind? Well, well! Surprise, surprise!" said Elechi as he began to walk away with his friends, leaving Reverend Harcourt both speechless and dumbfounded.

The conversation between the two ended as abruptly as it began, and none was angrier and more furious at the outcome than Mr. Gabriel Nnadiekwe, who was boiling with rage inside, towards Elechi and his friends, while he was interpreting the conversation to Reverend Harcourt. The two men looked at each other ashamedly without uttering a word, and Reverend Harcourt quietly walked away, as well, from the foul-mouthed man, as he later referred to him: a villager whom he had once considered innocent, naïve, a friend, and a true, soon-to-be convert. Not!

Chapter 12

The Eye-Opener

After that unfriendly encounter he had with Elechi Emewhule, Reverend Harcourt decided to sweep aside every feeling of innocence and naivety he had previously harbored for the natives. From now onwards, he was going to deal with them not as equals, but as one intent on converting the other. He was not going to be friendly with them, and he was not going to engage in any form of argument about God and the Bible with them. He was just going to tell them what he knows and what he thought they ought to know about God and that was that. They can either take it or leave it.

"What made you come to this conclusion?" asked Mr. Nnadiekwe, who was shocked by this impromptu announcement from his boss and confidant.

"Well, I think they know more than I thought they knew."

"Some of them, yes, but not all of them. At least not the majority," replied Mr. Nnadiekwe.

"But the few who knows are making it difficult for the many who don't know."

"And that is the whole point; that is why you are here."

"Why?"

"To help the many who do not know; to help them to know."

"I think you are right."

"You know I am, Pastor," said Mr. Nnadiekwe. "And what we must do is not to abandon the many that want to hear what you have to say for the sake of the few that feel that they know it already even though we all know they don't. Our message is for the many, not for the few that have long been lost to the devils. Those ones are lost and will never be found. They are dead and can never be resuscitated no matter how hard we try. They see no good in anything we are doing either here at school or at the mission. They believe in nothing, even though they claim to believe in everything, and they will let neither their children nor their wives learn as well. We are not after those few men and women; we are after the many lost souls that desperately need our help," concluded Mr. Nnadiekwe.

As they were having this conversation, one of the messengers came in and told Reverend Harcourt that someone wanted to see him.

"Who is it?"

"I don't know, sir," said the messenger.

"A man or a woman."

"A woman."

"Let her in, then." And in came Egbeke the wife of Weneka and the mother of the twins. She looked terrified and disheveled, and covered her face partly with her head-tie. As soon as she walked in, she fell on the ground in front of the two men and started sobbing profusely. Reverend Harcourt knew immediately who she was, for he had seen her the night the twins were brought back from the Evil Forest.

"Why are you crying, woman? Why?"

"Thank you, Pastor; I am here to thank you with all my heart."

"You don't have to, woman."

"Yes, I have to. You saved my life and that of my children."

"Thank you; but, please, stand up and sit down."

"Now, is it not too early for you to leave your house?"

"Pastor, I have not slept all night. In fact, I never slept since this incident happened."

The Victims of Rivalry

"Why?"

"I'm thinking about my children."

"Oh, don't worry about them … they'll be fine. They are with us now and they will be just fine. Trust me, they will."

"May I see them?"

"Of course, and you can see them anytime you want to. Remember, they are still your children. We are only protecting them from a brutal tradition, that's all. You can come here every morning and everyday to help them dress, eat, and get ready for church or school. As I said, we are holding them here for safekeeping, that's all. We are not holding them hostage."

"Thank you, Pastor."

"Don't mention it at all, woman; it is our pleasure to do it, to save the children of God from the mouth of evil. Now what name have you given them? Mr. Gabriel and I have given them the name Israel and Saturday, respectively. But I am sure you must have a native name for them."

"No, I don't, Pastor. It all happened so quickly. I didn't even have time to think, let alone think of names for them. But I can come up with names now if you want me to."

"Well, of course, you can come up with native names for your children. We already have English names for them. Unless you, of course, want us to schedule a naming ceremony at a later day."

"No! Not at all. You have done enough as it is. I can come up with native names now, if you don't mind."

"Then, do so."

"The one you call Israel I will call Manjor."

"Meaning what?"

"Meaning: I know no evil."

"Well, good!" said Reverend Harcourt. "Isn't that an appropriate name?"

"Indeed," replied Mr. Nnadiekwe, "quite befitting."

"Now what would you name the second one, Mrs. Weneka," asked Reverend Harcourt.

"The one you call Saturday I will call Nsijilem."

"Meaning?"

"Meaning: My ears are full."

"Full of what?"

"Full of gossips from neighbor and haters."

"Again, very good," said Reverend Harcourt. "You have done well, Mrs. Weneka. Those are good, thoughtful names. You are a lucky woman, and you have set a precedent. Many women in this village and beyond will thank you for what you have done. You have helped to save a whole generation of twins in this part of the world, only because you gave birth to your twins at the right time. Those children must live, and they deserve to live. Through them and through you, we have made history, and one that this village will never forget. Now you must excuse us. It is nearly 7:00 a.m., and we must start preparing for school. You can come here anytime to help us take care of your children. Our nurses are doing a fine job, but I think they can use your help. If you want, you can start today. In fact, you can go and see them now at the nursery." With these fine words to her eager ears, Egbeke rose up quickly to see her children. She had not seen them up close since the vigilantes snatched them from her mother's, their grandmother's, arms. And to behold them again after all this time was God-sent to her and she relished every moment of it.

After the rescue of Israel and Saturday, twins' rescue became an important part of Reverend Harcourt's mission in the village of Rumuachinva and, indeed, the entire Ovuordu clan. By the end of the year that the rescue operation began, the Baptist church and its sister Catholic church in the same village and surrounding villages had rescued over twenty twin births. And after much haggling by the villagers over whether or not it was the right thing to do, and after the fruitless speculation by the same villagers about what *Ohiomini* would do to those who are "taking food out of its mouth," the villagers accepted the fact that good had finally won over evil. As such, and from then onwards, the practice of throwing away twin children was finally abolished in the village of Rumuachinva and the entire clan of Ovuordu.

But there was more work to be done, Reverend Harcourt assured himself and made it his duty to remind Oha Achinike and his council of elders of his intentions.

"What exactly do you have in mind, Reverend Harcourt?" asked Oha Achinike, after Reverend Harcourt intimated to him that there was more work to be done to rid his village of the evil practices that have been holding its people back from accepting Jesus Christ as their savior.

"The worship of idols in your village is what troubles me," said Reverend Harcourt.

"What idols?" asked the Oha.

"The ones behind you," said Reverend Harcourt, pointing at the iron-clad ancestral staffs that stood planted on the ground behind the Oha, "the gods, and the so-called personal *chi* or god that the men in this village have erected by their bed sides.

"So what do you wish to do with them?"

"Cast them aside."

"*Tufia-yi!*" spat Oha Achinike, in disgust "And what would you do with them after you cast them aside?"

"Burn them."

"And you think burning them will bring our people in droves to your church?"

"Perhaps, it might."

"Well, I am sorry to say, I don't think so, Reverend Harcourt," said Oha Achinike. "You see, Reverend Harcourt, there are mountains you cannot move, there are rivers you cannot cross by walking or even sailing, and there are fires you cannot quench but must let alone to burn out on its own and at its own pace. Such mountain, such river, and such fire is this one that you are standing on. When you try to move these kinds of mountain, or try to quench these kinds of fire, or try to cross these kinds of river, they do not let you. They try to match your challenge with their own strength and legacy. If you win, they are reduced in the eyes of their peers around the world and in the eyes of those who revere them, and when they win over you, their fame and prestige is heightened among their peers and among those who believe in them.

"Now," continue Oha Achinike, "you may be wondering how I knew these things."

"Yes," replied Reverend Harcourt.

"Well, I don't, not literally. They are revealed to me secretly. Did you know that even mountains and rivers and fires brag about being impregnable and indestructible? Did you know that they have eyes and ears as we humans do? Did you know that these things that you thought were inanimate are truly animate and alive and well? Perhaps, you didn't know. But we in this village know these things. You have come to us with the knowledge of your God, whom we know to be *Chineke*. That is good, and we are glad. The truth is: He may be new to you, which is why you want to proclaim Him to the whole world, and that is good—very good of you, indeed. That is what we human beings do when we find something new and for the first time. We are infatuated and we want everyone else around us to know about it—that which we know or have discovered. Such discovery makes us feel good. That is, indeed, good of you, and it is human that you relish in sharing your new-find with others. Yet, I must tell you that this God that you claim to be proclaiming to us so-called gentiles and unbelievers is not new to us. He is our *Chineke*, and I will not be mistaken if I say that we have known Him, perhaps, far longer than you have. We know Him and we believe in Him. He is our creator and our maker. Not only is He a god, like all the other gods that we pay homage to in this village, He is the god that created. He created the other gods, and for that reason and much more, we respect and honor Him enough to acknowledge his presence everywhere and around us at all times.

"You see, Reverend Harcourt," continued the Oha, "our people have this proverb which I believe is appropriate and applicable here. They say: What the dog saw and started barking, the sheep had seen long ago and turned his face, pretending to be ignorant. The sheep saw what he saw and ignored it as though it didn't matter, even though it mattered and the sheep knew it mattered. But the dog saw it and started barking, acting as though he was the only one that saw something. He was not. This is exactly what I see here. Now what do I mean by that? Well, let us assume that we, my people and me, are the sheep. This news of your God, which happens to be new to you is not new to us. We have heard it before, and we know from whence it came. We just didn't make a big thing of it because we didn't have to. It is part of us and we are part of it. So why brag about what you are? That is not our way of doing things. That is not our way of reacting to good news or even bad news, for that matter!

"You and your people, on the other hand, are different," continued the Oha, "and there is nothing wrong in being different. In this case, however, you are the dog, and a dog cannot keep a secret. A sheep can. We heard this good news a long time ago. We knew it was good then, and we know that it is good today. We just didn't think it was necessary to run around the world screaming and shouting about the good news we heard, as if we were the only ones who have heard them. If you do that, you make yourself look foolish in the eyes of those who already knew what you just learned. The only thing you can gain from such hype is embarrassment. You even wrote down the news you heard and claimed that it was dictated to you by God. How? All this is just to make believe, and we in this village know these things.

"Now, I am not saying that you are embarrassed over what you are doing because I know you are not," added the Oha. "I can see that. I can see that you are awfully proud of what you are doing, and so are we for you. We are not a perfect people; I'm sure I've told you that before. But we have our pride, too. Contrary to what you think, our people do not worship idol, Reverend Harcourt," insisted the Oha. "We pay homage and we pour libations and we make sacrifices to our gods and our ancestor—the men and women who have lived this life before us and know the way of life on earth more than we can possibly know. We besiege them, so that they may guide and protect us from life's unforeseen circumstances. Now if you consider that worshipping idols, then so be it. We make no apologies nonetheless.

Continued Oha Achinike, "you have come a long way to show us some things we didn't know or, perhaps, knew but overlooked or took for granted. That is very good of you. We have accepted the changes in our tradition regarding twin children, and that is to your credit. That was made possible by your intervention, persistence, and foresight. We are thankful for that. There are many among my people, I believe, who would from henceforth abandon our ways to follow in your footsteps. I know that, and many have. They will even go as far as changing their native names, the names their fathers and mothers gave them. And there is nothing wrong with that. That is their choice and we respect their decision. Yet, there are certain of us, including myself, who are rooted in our culture and tradition and will die believing in those things that have kept us alive to this day. Those, my friend, I will urge you to stay away from if you want your mission here to be accomplished in peace. Take what you can and be thankful and do not be greedy, for greed will tame your heart as it has done many hearts, especially those who lust after it and do their utmost to shun due satisfaction!

"I am sure, Reverend Harcourt," continued the Oha, "that in where you come from, there are still people who do not believe in the new God you have found. I am quite sure of that. Don't ask me how I know that, but I do. And even if you tell me there is none, and that everyone in your nation believes in this your new-found religion, I will not believe you. And that does not mean you are a liar. After all, you are only being human—one wired with all the frailties that make us all humans! For, as human beings, we lie and we deceive ourselves and others in many ways. Perhaps you are not the eye-opener that you thought you were, after all. If anything I have said so far makes sense to you and to anyone who may be hearing it, it is simply that: God is your God; *Chineke* is our *Chineke*! Different names, one entity! If we all, no matter where you come from, can learn to live with that Almighty fact of life—you believing in what you believe and I believing in what I believe—I believe we will all live long and peacefully in the land which He had given us!"

Chapter 13

School Boom

The town crier boomed his metal gong late that evening. The deafening sound of the gong filled the air, and when all was silent, and he was sure that the crowd was quiet enough to hear him, he began to deliver his message.

"*Eeeee-yi, Rumuachinva!*
"*Eeeee-yi, Achinva dike!*
"*Eeeee-yi Eli-eli-dike!!*"
"*Achinva of brave warriors!*
"Listen carefully. *Nnewee-eli* and his council of elders have sent me to give you this message. As everyone knows, the White man's school at the Waterside is growing. Some of our 'strong' sons and daughter have now opted to go to the White man's school instead of our farms. That is not completely good news, but there is nothing we can do about it. They decided; we didn't make them decide; we didn't force them. What is happening, as you well know, is like a wind. A wind is blowing towards us, and there is nothing we can do to stop it, it seems. No one with his mind together can try to stop a wind if it really wants to blow. Attempts to stop a blowing wind have never yielded any good result. We have tried in our capacity to stop that wind by sending only our 'weak' children to the White man's school. But it seems that that is not working. Our 'strong'

children have now, for some reasons beyond our explanation, become jealous of our 'weak ones'. What they are jealous of, we do not quite know. But we will find out sooner or later, won't we? They, too, want to go to the White man's school to learn how to read and write. Because of this craze over the White man's knowledge, the Waterside school has ballooned overnight. Now the tide has turned. The White man, Reverend Harcourt, and his assistants need our help. They need more buildings, they need more play grounds, and they need our support. For the sake of our children and their future, the Oha and his council of elders have decided to act now before it is too late. For this reason, tomorrow, early in the morning, the Akwete age group and up to the Udokanma age group must report to the Waterside school to assist White man and his assistants in building new school houses and clear the bushes that surround the school. Anyone who fails to join his age group to partake in this call for action should be fined heavily by his age group; he should also be reported to the Oha for disobedience. Thank you."

The town crier's message was unusually long today. Most people didn't quite understand what he meant, but they caught on by inquiring from those who did, and the reaction from everyone was one of surprise and shock. "How can something once considered a punishment for the 'weak' children suddenly become a fashion for everyone overnight? What has gotten into the minds of the children of nowadays?" These were the questions that many asked that night, including a group of young men lounging around the village arena. "They no longer want to work; they just want to stay at that White man's school and do nothing all day," said one man.

"Yes, you are right," said another. "And they all want to be like him, too."

"Yes, they want to be lazy like him," said yet another. "They have no strength for farming and they have no strength for fishing."

"All they have strength for is talking."

"As if they can eat talking."

"And reading."

"And writing."

The Victims of Rivalry

"And now they want us to build new buildings for them."

"And cut their grasses, too!"

"Yes, and one day they will ask us to come and clean their toilet and their bottoms, too," said yet another, arousing laughter. They went on and on, and all the while they jabbed at the issue, they did not know that a young man whose parents considered "weak" and who was one of the pupils at the Waterside school was standing right beside them.

"Who told you we do nothing at the school, and that we are lazy?" queried the young man, whom Reverend Harcourt had nicknamed Simon, and whose native name was Ayiwe Wegumegu. He was not known for making trouble or to question his elders. But that night he was willing to risk his reputation and to do violence if necessary, in defense of his school.

"What do you do than sit around and lie to one another at that school?" responded the first man that spoke. The force of his response was not what Ayiwe had expected; he had expected a conversation. Instead he got a roar from a boar who valued nothing but his own opinion. But Ayiwe did not respond. He simply walked away as everyone was ganging up on him, knowing that his voice and his opinion can never make a dent in the minds of the "argumentative and good-for-nothing lot," as he later referred to them.

But the men did not stop there. They carried on with their argument and eventually decided to take their case to the entire village body. Initially it was just a handful of people who complained. Soon, however, the number of the disgruntled grew, and they found amongst them dissenters who were willing to go the extra mile to block what they felt was unfair to themselves and the majority of the natives, especially those who had been designated to work at the Waterside school.

They decided to lodge their case to the Oha and his council of elders. Once they were given audience, their spokesman, Elechi Emewhule, rose up and spoke these words: "How is it that we the hardworking men of this village—the ones who fish and farm—should abandon our day's work to support the White man's crazy ideas and lazy lifestyle? By letting our weak and lazy sons and daughter join him at the Waterside school, we believe that we have done enough for him. And what we had done, in our estimate, was the right thing to do—a necessary sacrifice of sort! Now, six years later, why is it that our good deed is coming back to bite us. Suddenly our 'strong' sons and daughters, who should be taking a liking to our farms and rivers, are instead taking a liking to the White man's lazy lifestyle and now the entire village is cowering into it and our leaders are agreeing, collaborating, and selling us whole. Why?"

Now, what these men and Elechi did not know and were soon to find out was that, just as the village had formed a habit of scrutinizing every new thing—be it goods or ideas—being introduced by anyone into the village of Rumuachinva, the Oha and his council of elders had done their homework in accordance with the philosophy of a proud, skeptical people. Long before they made the decision to assist the White man in expanding his school, they had asked him myriads of questions and he had answered them satisfactorily and without reservations. It was one of the rare moments Reverend Harcourt, in his estimate, had been asked to display his ingenuity in outwitting the native peoples, and he did not disappoint himself or the people who queried him. Hence, it could be said that the assimilation of the Black man into the White man's culture did not happen overnight in the village of Achinva. Reverend Harcourt drew his plan carefully and executed it as perfectly as anyone with sense would. And he couldn't have been happier with the way and manner with which it turned out!

It so happened that the Waterside school was not doing as well as Reverend Harcourt had wanted it to do. Although the school was functioning very well, it was not functioning at the vibrant pace that the Reverend had anticipated. And the reason, in his estimate, was because the entire village was not involved in it. In short, the heart and soul of the village was not in the school and that was not what he had wanted or had expected. He wanted better. He expected better. He wanted the village to own the school and for the school to be part of the village. He wanted the natives to be proud of the school and to call it their own, rather than the "White man's" own as was presently the case. He wanted the Waterside school to do better all year around and in every aspect, so he went to work and hatched out a plan of action. He began to think up things to do to spark the interest of the natives. He wanted them to send their more ambitious and motivated children to the school, as these, not the former, would bring the spark that the school need to jumpstart itself and triumph endlessly as he had first anticipated when he first arrived at the village of Achinva.

The first thing that came to his mind was to change the school uniform. The new uniform would be attractive to the eye and should command respect. The second thing was to buy more books for the small library he had established, as well as hire more qualified teachers to teach the school. And instead of asking the students to remove their uniforms and keep them at school before they went home, as was the practice, he would ask them to take them home with them. He would also ask them to take their books home and show their brothers and sister what they had learned at the school. He would also buy them sandals and white converses to wear in and out of school. In short, he would boost the pupil's "bragging rights" as a way of converting the hardheaded parents among the villagers. This was the plan he put to work one year ago, and it worked like a charm!

As events would have it, when the "weak ones" went home with their clean white shirts and black shorts, their sandals and white converses, and their book bags tucked on their side, they looked attractive and enviable. They were also instructed by their teachers and Reverend Harcourt to display all the things they had learned at the school. So the moment the pupils returned from school, they took out their books and pencils and began to write and to read whatever interested them at the watchful eyes of their "stronger" siblings. They would even write down their names using the English alphabet they had learned. What made this display even more fascinating and daunting to the villagers was that anyone of these kids could read what another had written, whether he was there when he or she wrote it or not. Because of this, rumor began to spread in the village that the White man was teaching the "weak ones" how to predict the future, how to perform magic, as well as how to read another's mind.

"How does he do that?" asked the Oha after he was told several stories of how the White man was brainwashing the children and teaching them how to predict the future and read minds, instead of learning how to read and write books, which was what he said his school was going to teach them. When Reverend Harcourt saw the messenger that had come to inform him that the Oha and his council of elders wanted to see him immediately two months after he had implemented his new tactics, he knew immediately and had a feeling that his idea had caught on.

"What have you been teaching the children?" asked Oha Achinike.

"How to read and write, as promised," responded Reverend Harcourt.

"But that is not what I heard."

"Oh, well, what have you heard?"

"I heard you are teaching the children how to predict the future and how to read minds and how to do magic."

"How?"

"You tell me."

"Well, I don't know what you mean, Your Highness."

"But is that what you are teaching the children?"

"How can that be? I don't even know how to do that myself. How can I teach someone what I don't know myself?"

"So you only teach what you know?"

"Yes, of course."

"And you don't know how to predict the future and read minds and do magic."

"No, I don't."

"Then why is everyone saying that you do."

"I don't know why, Your Highness."

The Victims of Rivalry

"Can you bring one of your pupils here and demonstrate what you teach them so I can see and hear?"

"Yes, indeed," said Reverend Harcourt, anxiously. "As a matter of fact I will bring five of them here right now and you can ask them any question. You can even ask them to write anything for you and they will do it. Ask them to write your names and to write a letter for you and they will do it in no time at all."

"Is that right," asked Oha Achinike, proudly. "You mean a son of Achinva can do all those things?"

"And more," bragged a beaming Reverend Harcourt.

"And more?" the Oha repeated after him and laughed out loud. "Then send for them." This agreement sent one of Reverend Harcourt's assistant rushing to the Waterside school. Within minutes, he returned with four neatly dressed boys and one girl. The five sat on a bench directly opposite the Oha. This was the closest any of them had ever come near the Oha and his council of elders, and, as any observer could see, the children were nervous. At first they were shaky and unsure of why they were there. But once Reverend Harcourt told them that they were there to display to the Oha and his council of elders what they had learned at the Waterside school, they eased up. To them, it was nothing. They had done it so many times that it had become second nature.

To start with, Reverend Harcourt asked each of them to read a passage from a book, and they read, to the amazement of the Oha and his council of elders, whose mouths were now almost agape with consternation. Then Reverend Harcourt asked each of the pupils to write down the names of the Oha and each of his council of elders, and they did. Then the Oha himself brought a letter he had recently received from the local government headquarters office, and they read and told him exactly what was in it. The five of them repeated this exercise one after the other. In the end, the Oha and his council of elders were convinced that Reverend Harcourt was teaching the children what every child of Rumuachinva ought to learn, not just the 'weak ones'. But a few amongst the elders were still not convinced. However, their opinions weighed little and could not prevent Oha Achinike from making a sweeping decision he felt was good for the future well-being of the children of Achinva. By the time the meeting ended, they had all made the decision to send some, if not all, of their own "strong" children to the White man's school as well, especially those who were willing and able.

This overwhelming approval of the Waterside school sparked a new interest in the school in the village of Rumuachinva and the neighboring villages. The following months brought about an enrollment of over two hundred percent from the previous years—a direct windfall from the display of confidence by the pupils, and "the triumph of knowledge over ignorance," using Reverend Harcourt's exact words. Reverend Harcourt had no choice but to expand the school. But he could not do it alone. Hence he solicited the help of the Oha and his council of elders, and they responded overwhelmingly, to the dismay and as well delight of the cunning and crafty White man!

"There are many ways to catch a monkey," he later said and rejoiced within himself, "and one of the ways is to give it wine, which it loves more than anything else in the world, and watch it crumble under its own weight!"

Chapter 14

A New Beginning

The expansion of the Waterside school brought with it more problems than solutions. Three more buildings had been erected, a football field had been carved out, a tennis court had been included, new teachers and teacher's aides had been hired, and the enrollment had ballooned beyond expectation. But before these things happened, Reverend Harcourt had assured the Oha and his council of elders and the parents of the pupils that his Mission would provide the pupils with uniforms, shoes, and writing materials. With these promises, the people were hooked on all the Reverend's burgeoning plans. And quite frankly, aside from the new buildings and the expansion of the school and the anticipation of all the good things the children would learn from the school, most parents willingly sent their children to the school and the children willingly went mainly because of the promises Reverend Harcourt had made them. Otherwise, they would not have gone and the Reverend knew it.

During this period in the village, clothes were scarce. Most pupils walked around naked because their parents could not afford to buy them clothes. But when a stranger comes out of nowhere to make a promise of providing that scarce clothes, and the only requirement was to make sure that the child woke up early in the morning to attend school, any parent, impoverished or not, would be thrilled. And that was exactly what happened when Reverend Harcourt made his promise. Parents were elated. In fact, they jubilated outdoors as would any happy African villager who encounters a fortune or appreciates the kindness of a stranger. Some even went personally to thank Reverend Harcourt and brought with them food produce or whatever they knew would bring comfort to a stranger among them, especially one that has demonstrated that he possessed a big, loving, and giving heart like Reverend Harcourt had. But what they didn't know as the year progressed was that they were in for a big surprise.

Initially, however, Reverend Harcourt was intent on making good on his promise. But as the school year progressed and more and more pupils enrolled, he began to have a second thought and then finally aborted the idea altogether from the list of the things he had promised to do for the pupils. Two months into the school year and still the parents did not see the much anticipated changes in clothing that Reverend Harcourt had promised them and their children. Although the children were learning, and the school was in full progress, some of the pupils went to school either half-dressed or outright naked. At this point some of the parents began to wonder and to speculate that the White man has, again, deceived them. But while these doubting Thomases were still speculating, Reverend Harcourt decided it was time to implement his plan B.

"Go home and tell your parents to give you your school fees," he told the pupils one early morning at the assembly.

"What?" shouted the pupils and some of the teachers and their aides, who were not informed of the changes before harmed.

"Yes, school fees," repeated Reverend Harcourt. "Running the school is now becoming a burden to the church. Our school has grown larger than I had anticipated and at a faster pace. As such we can no longer run the school without running it aground. We need money, and the only way we can raise that money is by asking you pupils to ask your parents to pitch in. Only the Weak Ones, the pioneers of this school would not be required to pay, but the rest of you must pay some form of school fees. The exemption of the Weak Ones also includes a free supply of books and uniforms. The rest of you will be supplied these things upon paying your school fees of five shillings each. So go now to your parents and make sure to return with your fees. If you do not have your fees, do not return." The pupils and some of the teachers and assistants looked at each other and could not believe what they were hearing. But the order had been given, and there was no going back.

Within hours, however, the gates of the Waterside school were flooded with parents. But neither Reverend Harcourt nor any of his teachers were willing to come out and speak with them. So they took their complaints to the Oha and his council of elders, whose children had also been sent home to collect school fees. Reverend Harcourt was summoned to explain the reason for his broken promise.

"What has suddenly become of your school, Reverend Harcourt, that it has turned into a mad house?" asked Oha Achinike.

"A mad house?"

"Yes, that is what I hear, a mad house."

"Well, I don't think so, Your Highness."

"Why don't you think so?"

"I am just coming from there now and there is nothing mad about the place."

"Then why can't the children stay in it?"

"Is that what they told you?"

"Why not go right to the point and explain to us why you have decided to step back from the promise you made to us here. You promised the children uniforms, shoes, and books if they came to your school. Now the children have our permission and they are now willingly coming in droves to your school and your reward for our change of heart is to ask us to pay for their studies and for their uniforms and shoes. Why?"

"I can explain, Your Highness."

"Go on, explain."

"First of all, Your Highness, I did not expect this many pupils to turn up. Frankly, I am thrilled that the school has grown, yet I am overwhelmed by the number."

"And so are we," interrupted Oha Achinike.

"But it is I who must do something about it."

"And what do you plan to do?"

"What I had already done."

"Which is?"

"Ask the parents to support their children."

"Was this our original agreement?"

"No, Your Highness."

"Then, why the change of heart?"

"No, it is not a change of heart, Your Highness; it is rather a change of circumstance."

"What is the difference?"

"One is deliberate; the other bears upon chance."

"And chances were that, we, the parents may be required to pay for sending our children to your school."

"No, the chances are now, not before; whether chances were then was not anticipated. I am, indeed, overwhelmed by the number of pupils. I want you to understand my position, Your Highness. Were the number smaller, we would have managed. But they are not. We need your help; the school needs your help to stay alive. And we are begging you to assist us. Help us so we can help the children!"

"You see, Reverend Harcourt, in this world, a little humility goes a long way," said Oha Achinike. "The elephant may be large and intimidating, yet it still has to respect the rat. You know why?"

"No, Your Highness."

"I will tell you, and I want you to listen carefully to what I have to say. Perhaps it might help you as you troupe around the world and come into contact with different peoples and different cultures and traditions. You see, my son, it takes a little rat to humiliate a large elephant. The elephant may be huge, but a rat can embarrass it if it decides to flaunt its size and take the rat for granted. Now, why am I saying this? We may be a small village, and you may have all your mighty church and your mighty Queen behind you, but you are no match to us when we make up our minds to do something. When we decide to do something, this little village does it with pride and dignity, and efficiently as well. Sometimes it is not that you asked for something that matters, it is the manner in which you ask it that matters. It is my profound belief that you deliberately decided to embarrass this village. Otherwise you would not make a decision, in direct violation of a promise you made to us here not long ago, without consulting with us, the custodians of this village.

"Were I to rush to anger," continue the Oha, "I would have rushed to judgment and asked you to pack up and leave my village. But I am slow to anger, and so are my people. We will not ask you to leave, unless you want to. This is because we keep our promise. We have made you a promise, and we intend to keep it. But you have decided to break yours, and for a reason which is quite understandable, based, as you said, on circumstances which we now know to be financial.

"But we are an understanding people," continued the Oha. "And all you would have done is come to me and my council of elders and explain the predicament that you are in and we will see to it that you are bailed out in the same manner that this village does its things: expeditiously and timely. But to send our children out of your school is nothing short of insulting us. And I, for one, I am humiliated that my own children were sent away. That, my friend, is not the way we do things in this little village of ours. Our people have pride, we have dignity, and we intend to keep it that way!

"We will help you out, stranger!" said the Oha. "We will agree to pay the school fees you have proposed, and we will help your school to grow and prosper. Do you know why?"

"No, I don't, Your Highness."

"Well, I'll tell you," said the Oha. "The reason I am telling you we will help you with a certain degree of certainty even without consulting with my people is because I see this school not as your school but as the school of this village. We now own this school because it is in our village and we will do whatever it takes to keep it open for our children's sake and for the sake of their future. The future of this village concerns me."

"I couldn't have expressed it any better, Your Highness" said Reverend Harcourt. "And I thank you very much for your understanding."

"Don't mention it. Now go home and we will get back to you. If there is anything, anything else at all that you want of us or need from us, let us know. We are here for you and we are here for our children—never forget that!"

Chapter 15

The Communal Spirit

When Oha Achinike and his council of elders told Reverend Harcourt "we will help you out," the White man didn't know exactly what they meant, yet he never asked. He was content with their response, and simply accepted their not dismissing his proposal outright as a victory. What he didn't know, however, was that the villagers were about two steps or more ahead of him. They wanted good things for their children, and if educating them in the White man's school was what it would take to make the children happy and progressive, they were willing to do just that—whatever it is!

But there was one thing Reverend Harcourt said that they did not particularly like. And that one thing was that only those children whose parents can afford to pay their school fees could attend the Waterside school. They did not like that proposal for two reasons. One, such is not an aspect of their communal character. Second, it will expose their village as one that has a gutter between haves and have-nots, and that is simply unacceptable; for, in their eyes, everyone has, and those who do have more must be readily willing to share with those who do not have enough. "Perhaps that is the way they do things in where he comes from," said one of the elders whose name was Ezekwe Omeoka.

"It must be," said another.

"That man strikes me as strange, anyway, and his proposal was no different," said yet another.

"Why?" asked Oha Achinike. "Why do you say such things about him? He seems quite sincere to me. Perhaps, as Omeoka suggested, that is the way they do things in his home country."

"But I have reasons for saying what I said," responded Ottamini Ndike.

"Which is?" asked Oha Achinike.

"Well, his own wife died and he never shed a tear; that is one thing."

"How do you know that?"

"That is what I heard."

"How many times have I told you to stop hearing things?" said Oha Achinike. "Hearing things brings troubles always, I have often warned you. If you only heard it and you were not there to see or experience it, keep it to yourself. Chances are that it did not happen as you heard. And when the truth of what actually happened is exposed, what does that make you?"

"A liar," uttered someone.

"True," agreed Oha Achinike. "Now, kindly tell us how such thoughts could have crept into your head when we are discussing something more important as our children's future? A time for a joke is a time for a joke. When we are discussing something as important as our children's future, no one should reduce it to a joke. Now, where were we?"

"We were talking about the White man's proposal," said Ezekwe Omeoka, who was most eager to change the subject.

"Yes, indeed," said Oha Achinike, "and that is what we should be talking about and nothing more. The children of this village deserve better. In fact, they all deserve the same thing. Think about it for a moment. How can it be that some of them got this education because their parents can afford it and others did not because their parents cannot? What type of society would that make us?"

"A society of rich and poor," said Omeoka.

"But is that really who we are?"

"Not at all," responded Omeoka.

"Is that the type of image to portray of ourselves?"

"No," answered Ottamini.

"Then what should we do? Omeoka, do you have any suggestions? Anyone?" inquired the Oha.

"Actually, I do," murmured Omeoka.

"Then say it, and say it aloud," growled Oha Achinike amusingly to soft-spoken Omeoka's serious disposition.

"As you hinted a few minutes ago," said Omeoka, "I think we should approach the White man's proposal with caution."

"How do you mean?"

"I mean so we do not do things we will regret in the future."

"Good—. So what should we do?"

"I think his proposal is good, and it makes a lot of sense. Instead of the school to fold up and close, I think we, the people of this village, should assist in keeping it open, especially since we now know and believe, after our recent inquiry of the gods, that the future of our children depends on it. We don't know exactly what this means. But if the gods are right as we all know they often are, then this is not a matter to be taken lightly."

"Then what are you suggesting?" demanded Oha Achinike somewhat impatiently.

"I am suggesting that we approach it as a community; I am suggesting that we solve it the way we solve our communal problems. If we leave it in the hands of parents alone, many of our young ones will not benefit. Some parents have more than five children, and most may not afford to educate all of them. The White man has done us some good by taking the burden of the "Weak Ones" out of us. Now, it is our turn to show him what we are truly made of, and that we care about our children and our community."

"So what are you suggesting?" interrupted Ottamini.

"Will you let me finish?" uttered Omeoka irritably.

"Then finish quickly!" said Ottamini.

"Are you trying to hurry me?"

"No, but you are talking too much."

"But I am talking sense; I am talking about the problem at hand."

"Then say what you have to say and sit down."

"Are you trying to insult me?"

"What insult?"

"Enough!" interrupted Oha Achinike. "We need not quarrel about this issue. Omeoka has not finished what he had to say, so let him finish. Everyone one of us will have his turn to speak. This is his turn. So let him speak his mind, no matter how long it takes him. He may end up speaking for all of us, we don't know. But we must lend him our ears." With this shore of support, Omeoka rose up again and began to speak, picking up from where he had left off.

"What separates us from other people is our ability to speak and act as one, even in moments of crises," continued Omeoka. "You see, when I was young, only but a lad, my mother told me a proverb. It has been a long time since she told me these words, and up until now that I stand here before you, every bit of it still rings true in my ears. She said: 'The rain supplies water and the eye supplies water as well. But all my life I have never known anyone who relies on the water supplied by the eyes for their livelihood: I have never seen anyone collect it for cooking, and neither have I seen anyone collect it for drinking.'

"Now why did I remember these words on this auspicious moment that may perhaps decide the future of our children in a world that the gods have told us is about to change—about to explode before our own very eyes! We don't know whether the change is for the better or whether it is for the worse. Yet we know that there will be a change, and that the change is inevitable. Why? Because the gods have spoken it. That is why. And I believe them, just as everyone of you believe them. Lucky for us, we have a choice. We have a choice now. We have a choice between knowledge and ignorance, and our children are watching. They are watching to see which one we would choose.

"As every one of you knows, I am not all-knowing, and neither is any one of us here. Yet, I know some things. And, most importantly,

I am willing to share what I know. Unlike some people, I am not stingy with my ideas. I believe in this community, I believe in this village in particular, and I believe that my ideas are public property, which is why I am willing to share them publicly.

"As I was saying before I was rudely interrupted, I don't know what is in the heart of the White man, and neither do any of us. But whatever it is that is on his mind, we have seen some proof that he has no bad intentions. If he did, the gods would have, no doubt, alerted us, and they would have ousted him by now. We have seen proof of some of his work in this community. So far, his work has been good. He has proven to us his worth by teaching some of our children, especially the Weak Ones, how to read and write and we have seen proof of that. Since we have no reason to believe that he has any bad intentions, based on his work, I think we should open up and help him help our children."

"What are you suggesting, then?" asked Oha Achinike.

"Are you asking the type of help we should give him?" inquired Omeoka.

"No, that much we know; we know he needs financial help. I guess my question is: how do we go about raising money to help the school?"

"Well, that is not for us to decide here; that is for the people to decide."

"Then we should take our case to the people."

"Indeed, we should," affirmed Omeoka. "Our duty here is to decide whether or not we, the guardians of Rumuachinva, wish to help the school. Since I hear no objection, then we should take the case to the people. They are the ones that will be tasked to contribute their hard-earned money, and they are the ones that will make the final decision on the matter."

"I think you are right," said Oha Achinike.

"But what if they refuse?" asked one of the elders.

"Then it cannot be done," replied Omeoka. "But their refusal, based on my sampling of a few people I know personally, is unlikely."

"Let us hope so," said Oha Achinike.

"Indeed," sighed Omeoka to end his long speech. Within seconds, the meeting was over and every man his home went. A few days later the entire village was assembled in the Arena of the First Sons. The multitude was large, including men, women, and children. They did not know exactly what they had been assembled for, but some people had an idea and were voicing out their opinion as loudly as they could to the people standing next to them. As the assembly grew, it did not take long before the village orator Mgbechi "Onuoha" Okwele, the mouthpiece of the Oha, stood on a podium before the people of Achinva.

"*Rumuachinva, meka!*"

"*Iyeah!*" *roared the people.*

"*Meka!*"

"*Iyeah!*"

"*Meka!*"

"*Iyeah!*"

"*Meka!*"

"*Di eli!*"

"Thank you for coming, every one of you," bellowed Onuoha. "We have been assembled here by the Oha and the council of elders. They have told me something to tell you. What I am about to tell you now are not my words. They are not my thoughts either. They are what I have been told to tell you. So lend me your ears.

"As every one of you knows by now, a wave of change is blowing through our village. Some of our children can now read and write. I am sure you will all agree that that is a good thing. I personally believe that it is a good thing, and the Oha and his council of elders believe also that it is a good thing. And no one can doubt what our children think about all these changes. If you have children, I am sure you know how excited they feel. However, amid that change has arisen a challenge, and that challenge is a test of our will—the will of the people of this august village. The challenge is whether or not we want the Waterside school to continue to exist and operate in our village. If we don't want it, other villages are eager and willing to relocate it. Do we want it to remain open in our village or do we want it to relocate to another village? That is the question, and that is the challenge! The Oha and his council of elders met a few days ago to discuss this matter and to answer to the challenge. After much haggling and negotiating, they all agreed that it is in our children's as well as our village's best interest to keep the Waterside school open in our village. It is your turn, therefore, as the ultimate decider, to approve or disprove what your leaders have already approved. Now, the question before you is: Do we want the school open or do we want its doors closed in our village?"

"We want it to remain open," roared the crowd.

"Did I hear you want it to remain open?" asked Onuoha.

"Yes, we want it to remain open," the crowd responded enthusiastically.

"Well then, as you said, it will remain open. But I must warn you, there is no going back once you have agreed and endorsed it."

"We are not going back on our words," roared the crowd again.

"If you insist that the school must remain open, then I have no choice but to tell you the price for keeping it open."

"Go ahead, tell us," responded the crowd.

"I must warn you now that it will cost you your yams and your cassavas, your banana and your plantains, your penny and your pounds, your fish and your meat. Now, after hearing this, do you still want the school to remain open?"

"No!" shouted some louder than everyone else.

"Yes!" shouted others.

"I hear some people say 'no'. And I hear some say 'yes'. But a few minutes ago, those who are saying 'no' now said 'yes'. Now, that is not the spirit of our people. We do not give our words and then take it back, do we?"

"No!" roared the crowd.

"Then we must make up our minds and do the right thing. The Waterside school is in deep financial trouble. As a result, the white Man who runs it, Reverend Harcourt, wants to close it and return to his home country or relocate it to another village willing and able to support it. We can let him go or we can contribute money to assist him to keep the school open. That is the choice we have to make, and that is the true reason why you have been assembled here this morning. The Oha and the council of elders have taught about it and had agreed that assisting the white man to assist our children is the best thing to do. Now they want to know what you, the people, think. It is now your turn to voice your opinion. And I must remind you that your opinion alone is the only one that will count here, for it is you who will contribute the money, not just the Oha and his council of elders. All of us are in this together as one. And so as is our tradition when making an important decision of this magnitude, the Oha has instructed me to tell you to split yourselves in groups, however you choose—either according to age groups, according to families, or according to political leanings. This is an opportunity to chat among yourselves, agree to disagree, and then report back to the Oha. We have all day ahead of us, so take your time while not thinking of time! You may choose to sit here in circles under the cotton trees, or you may go to your various gathering places, but we must all reassemble here at sundown to hear the yields of your thoughtful minds."

"You have spoken well," yelled a voice in the crowd as the people decided on how to split up themselves.

"Yes, you are truly the 'Onu' of the Oha," yelled another, sarcastically, arousing lots of laughter among the crowd. Suddenly a sense of duty and obligation descended up the people of Achinva, for they do not give in easily to challenge. Soon after Onuoha's speech, the villagers split into various age groups. Each group then sort a suitable place to chat away the time. Some sort a more suitable place to have their conference, and others merely sat under a tree. Soon, however, the center of the arena was empty, and its content eaten whole by the village corners and crannies.

Outwardly, the villagers seemed acquiesced, but the Oha and his council of elders would have been fools if they thought that the matter was decided. They knew better, and they knew that their village was laden with skeptics, and these rabble-rousers would never accept anything for granted. And it did not take long

The Victims of Rivalry

before the skeptics voices began to be heard among their various age groups.

"Why," asked Elechi Emewhule "do we have to contribute money to support the White man?"

"No, Elechi, you are getting it all wrong," said Onuoha, who is not only the village orator but also a member of Igwuruve age group to which Elechi belongs.

"How? How I am getting it wrong?"

"The money is to help the White man help our children."

"Who invited him to come and help our children?"

"No one."

"No one, right?"

"Yes, Elechi, no one invited him to come to our village," said Onuoha.

"Now he wants to scan us for some money and you rulers of this village are so blinded that you cannot see. You think you can just tell us the White man needs this and that and we will say, yes, here, have it. Well, it will not work. I am against it. I am against giving the White man anything. After all, we did not invite him here. He came by himself."

"But he came to help us."

"What do you mean? He came to help us do what?"

"To educate us and our children."

"To educate who? You?" blared Elechi. "Are you not educated? Oh, I didn't know you were not educated," he mocked. "Well, that is you. As for me, I am quite educated and I don't need the White man's education. We rejected his ideas first when he first proposed it to us, which was why we gave him the 'weak ones' to give his so-called education. Now he has used his chameleon-style entry to penetrate us and we are falling like a helpless tree under the spell of a mindless wind god. We are smitten by his charm. He has sent the 'weak ones', the people whom we regarded as nothing because they have no strength to work and to grow food and to fish, to woo our children and our people's minds. His magic has worked on our children. Now you elders and leaders of this village have fallen for him, too. But this man, Elechi," he pointed to himself, "cannot be fooled. Before the dawn arrived, the cocks knew it was coming; it was just a matter of time. But I am not one to be fooled!"

"But you are not the only one making the decision," retorted Onuoha.

"You are right I am not."

"And you cannot overrule the decision of the majority."

"No, I cannot; but I can refuse to make any contribution, can't I?"

"And risk being banished from our village?

"So what? So what if I am banished from this village. There are many villages that will open their arms to me."

"You really think so?"

"Why not?"

"Not if they truly know you?"

"Are you trying to insult me, Ohuoha?"

"No, Elechi, you are insulting yourself." These types of argument went on among the age groups, but none was as violent and as interesting as that of Agwuruve age group, and, with Elechi among them, it was hardly unexpected. As the day wore on and evening approached and the shadows of trees elongated, exposing its shade to sunlight, the villagers trickled back into the arena. By total sundown, the arena was full again, and, once more, at the podium, stood Ohuoha. Before he rose up to speak, however, each leader of the age group had reported the group's decision to the Oha and his council of elders and each of their decisions had been passed on to Onuoha. So, as he stood, he was armed with the people's verdict.

"Rumuachinva anu meka!" bellowed Onuoha.

"Di eli!" replied the multitude.

"Meka!"

"Di eli!"

"Meka!"

"Di eli!"

"Meka!" "Di eli!"

"Well, you have spoken. And, according to the Oha, you have spoken well. You have agreed to assist the White man. You have agreed to help him help our children. The Oha and the council of elders have asked me to thank you. You have done well, and they are pleased with your decision. As they say, we thank a philanthropist not just for what he had done today, we thank him for what he will do tomorrow, and next tomorrow! Today you have done well. As such, we know you will do well tomorrow also. The Oha thanks you! And the elders thank as well.

"Now, it is not enough to say we will do something. If it were so, many among us here would have become wealthy. What counts is what we actually do, not just what we say we will do. We have agreed to assist the White man's school; let us now agree on how we will actually go about doing it. On this aspect, you have thought long and hard, the Oha and the elders have also thought long and hard, and we have come to an agreement, based on our consensus conclusions.

"What we have agreed to is simple and makes a lot of sense. We have rich people among us, and we have poor people among us. This is true, and there is nothing wrong in that. Everyone does not become rich, and everyone in a village is not poor. There is always a mix, and that is good, as everyone takes pride in being who he or she is. A land that has no rich people is like a people without leaders, and a land that has no poor people is like leaders that have no people to lead. But our village has both, and for that we are blessed. Based on your decision, the Oha and his council of elders want every able man in this village to contribute ten shillings each every *eke* day, which is our market day. Those who cannot afford the money can contribute a bunch of plantain or banana or two yams or a basin of cassava tubers. These items will then be sold at our village market or sent to Rumuedo market for sale. The proceeds will be put in our treasury, which we will dip into to assist the White man to run the Waterside school. Those who can afford it, that is the rich ones among us, and they know themselves, can contribute more and as they please, but not less than the rest.

"This money will not be wasted, and it will not be given to the White man to keep for us. It is our money and we will appoint a treasurer and a group of people who knows how to count money to work with this person. This will bring about checks and balances and leave nothing unchecked and no decision regarding how the money will be spent unchallenged.

"The White man came to our village without our knowledge. We all know that. Whatever was in his mind before he came, we do not know. But upon allowing him to stay among us, we have discovered that his intentions are not malicious. We have also discovered, based on what he told us and from what we ourselves can see, that his school has grown. His once deep pocket has suddenly become shallow as a result of the increase in enrollment in that school. We have agreed to deepen that pocket somewhat. However, we are not suggesting that we will shoulder all the responsibilities of that school. That would be putting too much on our shoulders. Just because the squirrel saw the kernel and chewed it to prevent the kernel from getting rotten or wasted does not mean that its stomach should rot. Nothing of that sort will happen at all. The White man will continue to run his school with his own money. We will merely relieve him of some of the financial burden. We will match every penny that his country or church leaders give him, and we will do whatever it takes to keep our children happy and educated. *Nkalem anu meka!*" said Onuoha before he bowed to the crowd and exited the podium.

"*Onu-oka*," meaning artistic mouth, shouted someone in the crowd as the villagers began to disperse. By now the arena had turned, literally, into a market place. Some heaped praises at Onuoha for being so artistic in convincing the people with his tricky ways of presenting the ideas of the Oha and his council of elders. Others thought otherwise. They thought he was merely an agent of deception and there was nothing artistic about his ploy. The main proponent of this later school of thought was, of course, Elechi, the skeptic and rabble-rouser.

"What is making all of you so happy?" he questioned the people around him in disgust. "Is it because the White man had come all the way from wherever he came from to twist our arms and we are falling wholesale for his trap? Don't you people have senses? Can't you think?"

"Think about what, Elechi?" queried Onuoha, who had tracked Elechi down immediately after his speech, to hear what he had to say about the whole thing. Although Elechi is known throughout the village of Achinva as a skeptic and trouble-maker, he is also considered one of the great thinkers, for some of his thoughts are right on. Yet, most of the time, his thoughts, good and intelligible as they may sound, are made insignificant by his loud mouth and uncontrollable fits of skepticism and sudden burst into unnecessary argument.

"That arm-twisting you did there," replied Elechi.

"What arm-twisting?"

"You call that a speech? What you did there you call it a speech?"

"What else can you call it?"

"Lies—pack of lies."

"What lies? I was only telling the people what the Oha and the council of elders said. I wasn't twisting anybody, was I?"

"Do you really want me to answer that question?"

"Yes, indeed, answer it. Whose arms did I twist?"

"Ours—all of us—including yours—"

"How? How did I do that?"

"You don't know?"

"No, I don't."

"And you want me to tell you?"

"By all means, please tell me."

"Well, I am not going to tell you anything. I am not going to tell you what I know you already know. Go home and sleep on it. Perhaps it will pop up in your dream and you and the entire village will finally come out of your slumber. By then it would have been too late, and you will have no one but yourselves to blame!"

"Is that your prayer, Elechi?"

"No, it is your unbeknownst wishes for this village and its future!"

Chapter 16

The Chosen Ones

Reverend Harcourt was pleased with the generosity of the people of Achinva. As such, he accepted their proposals without asking too many questions. He agreed to their bid to match his budget penny for penny, the proceeds of which will be used to improve the Waterside school. The school had grown significantly, as even neighboring villages were sending their own children to the refurbished school. Some children were trekking up to twenty miles or more to come to the Waterside school because it was the only one closest to them. The teachers were proud of the pupils, especially their level of curiosity and their desire to learn. They were not surprised, however, that the pupils preferred coming to school than engaging in the arduous and rigorous farming and fishing activities that were going to be their imposed professions. They saw relief in the eyes of the children, and this relief, they thought, was evidence of a brighter future for the village of Achinva.

No one saw this brighter future more clearly than Reverend Harcourt himself. Because either side had fulfilled its promises of keeping the school afloat financially, the pupils progressed academically, even beyond Reverend Harcourt's expectations. In fact, by the sixth year of the school's inception, some of the pupils, especially the pioneers of the school, the "weak ones," could now

The Victims of Rivalry

read and write fluently. Some, like Simon Wegumegu and Peter Amadioha could do arithmetic, algebra, and even more advanced mathematics. And so on the seventh anniversary of the school's inception, a year after the pioneers graduated, Reverend Harcourt made a startling announcement to the Oha and his council of elders.

"I will be going on my annual vacation within the next few days," he said. "But this time I will not be going alone."

"Who is the lucky woman?" asked Oha Achinike.

"No, it not a woman, and it is not one person."

"Then who might these lucky people be?"

"They are your children—the children of Achinva."

"Our children?"

"Yes, your children."

"You mean you will be taking the sons or the daughters of the village to the land of the White man?"

"Yes."

"And when will that be?"

"When I go on my vacation this year—in a few days."

"And who might these children be? Who are those lucky sons and daughters of ours?"

"They are two exactly."

"And who are they?"

"Simon Wegumegu and Peter Amadioha."

"That is good of you."

"Thank you."

"But those are the 'weak ones'. Wouldn't you be better off taking much more promising children to the land of the White man? After all, whoever you take is going there to represent us, and I don't think anyone in this village would want the 'weak ones' to represent us anywhere, right?" he asked, looking in the direction of his council of elders. "Although they are our children, these people do not quite represent the energy of this village. We thought we convinced you about this long ago," said Oha Achinike.

"Indeed, we did—," responded Omeoka.

"But those two are the best and the brightest that the school can boast of right now," injected Reverend Harcourt. "And besides, they are going to represent the Waterside school, too, not just the village of Achinva. If they do well, the honor and the glory will go out not to the village alone, but also to the school."

"I think you are right," said Oha Achinike.

"I know I am right, Your Highness," assured Reverend Harcourt. "Although you call them the 'weak ones', based on their performance in your village activities, I call them the 'bright ones', based on their performance in the school activities. They have proven that it does not take physical strength to perform well academically. These two lads are among the first group of pupils that started in our school, and they have gained more knowledge and experience as a result. They may not have the physical prowess, which your tradition demands of farmers and fishers, but they do have the brain power, which the school demands. This is why I have chosen them.

"Perhaps, in due course, the ones you consider the best representatives of your village, your so-called best and brightest, who joined the school later, will advance their studies later in England, but not until they have proven themselves and have gained the knowledge and experience necessary for a higher academic pursuit."

"Well said," said the Oha. "So, now, tell us, what will these young men be doing for you in your home country?

"For me?"

"Yes, for you."

"Nothing."

"You mean they are going there to do nothing?"

"No, they are not going there for me; they are going there to study."

"Are they not studying in the school here?"

"Yes, they are. But the type of higher knowledge they need this school can no longer provide."

"Why?"

"It is hard to explain."

The Victims of Rivalry

"Well, try; we would want to know. If you are going to take our sons and daughter across the ocean to go to school when there is a school here, we would want to know why."

"The reason is simple," said Reverend Harcourt. "They need higher knowledge than we can provide here due to our limited resources."

"So they have read all the books you have here."

"Something like that, yes."

"*Ewu!* So they have to go the place where the books are made to read some more."

"Something like that, yes?"

"So those children are that good."

"I'm afraid to admit it, but yes."

"*Ewuuu!*" lamented Oha Achinike. "Let the gods guide them. Let them take our children to the land of the White man and guide and protect them while there. Let your people assist them as we are assisting you here."

"Amen!" said Reverend Harcourt.

"So when are you planning to leave?" asked Oha Achinike excitedly.

"In a few days."

"Then you could have told us earlier—at least a week earlier so we can prepare."

"Prepare for what."

"For your send-off party."

"I don't need a send-off party, and neither do the kids. Yes, you are right, I could have informed you earlier. It just never occurred to me to do so."

"Why not?"

"I cannot say. Anyway, now that I think of it, I think I should have informed you earlier."

"Indeed, you should have," said Oha Achinike. "But what is done is done. Now, tell us, how may we assist you in making your travel easy, and our children's stay there worthwile? In short, what sort of assistance do you need from us?"

"A lot," replied Reverend Harcourt as a matter-of-factly.

"*Eh*, like what?"

"Money, of course," said Reverend Harcourt. "The children will need nothing more than money, but I am reluctant to ask it."

"Why?"

"Because you have done so much for the school already."

"And we will do some more if it is for the good of our village and our children," assured Oha Achinike.

"That is very nice of you, Your Highness," replied Reverend Harcourt. "Yet, I remain hesitant to tell you what it will take. The financial burden might break the back of this village, and you and your people will hate me for it. I do not want to go that far."

"But we would not want our children to suffer in a foreign land; we would not want them to go there and beg for something we can provide here. Tell us what is on your mind, and if we cannot fulfill it we will tell you without hesitation."

"Well, I like your kindness and the kindness of your people. Even though what I am doing is for your own good and for your brighter future, I still believe that it my burden to bear. Last week I asked the government of Nigeria for scholarships for these two boys to study abroad, but they turned it down. These are bright kids, and I believe your village desperately needs the likes of them if you anticipate a brighter future in a fast changing world."

"What is *colasifu*?"

"Oh, scholarship; it is government's financial assistance for people studying abroad."

"Do they give it to a lot of people?"

"Yes."

"Have they given it to anyone you know?"

"Yes, indeed, quite plenty I might add."

"And you asked them to give it to our two boys and they refused?"

"Yes, they turned them down, and I don't know why. They wouldn't tell me why. It is not because of academic ineptitude on the part of the boys; I don't think so. Those boys are as qualified and as able as anybody academically. But they turned them down. The reason, I don't know."

"Then ask them no more," said Oha Achinva somewhat angrily. "This village must bear her troubles alone. It had always done so, and it will continue to do so. We do not seek help from anyone, and whatever it is that you need to support these boys, we will provide—be it money, be it food, be it books. If you ask and we do not have, we will work hard and provide it.

"What you have told us here today, Reverend Harcourt, is a thing worthy of celebration, and we will celebrate it. Go back to your home and relax. Give us some time to talk things over with our people, and we will get back to you in a day or two. But be not discouraged. Knowing our people as I know them, this new challenge is ours to confront and conquer. Ours is the land of the gods and brave ancestors. We do not shy away from problems, and neither do we make vain promises or let obstacles hinder our resolve. We don't have much, but the little we have we share with one another. So, go home and you will hear from us within a day or two."

Chapter 17

Educating the People

Oha Achinike sent for Reverend Harcourt early one morning. When the Reverend arrived at the court of the Oha, he was alarmed by the crowd of people surrounding it. It was as though the entire village had been assembled. Yet, it was nothing of the sort. No one had sent for the villagers, not the Oha and his council of elders, and not the town crier. They came because they heard, from one mouth to the other, what Reverend Harcourt had told the Oha and his council of elders about taking the two boys overseas for further studies. Some of the villagers did not believe it. And so they wanted to hear it from the horses' mouth, as they say, and they wanted to know why Reverend Harcourt had chosen the "weak ones" and not the ones they considered the future and the brightest sons of Achinva—the "strong ones." Leading this group of inquisitors was none other than Elechi Emewhule and the mere onlookers he calls his friends.

But the Oha and his council of elders did not want to haggle over the matter any longer, at least not in the face of the entire village. This was why he had sent for Reverend Harcourt to come to his court. Even the Oha was surprised to see that many people in his compound. However, he was not enraged. Rather than be angry, he welcomed their wishes to hear from the source what he had already acclaimed to be good news for the village of Achinva.

As if he knew why Oha Achinike had sent for him, Reverend Harcourt went with the two boys in tow. No one could doubt that the boys were in shock as well to find that many people at the palace of the Oha so early in the morning, for it showed in their faces. But there was nothing they or anyone could do about it. Soon, however, their bewilderment turned into laughter as Oha Achinike, upon seeing them, began to shower praises upon them.

"Blessed be the gods for our sons and our daughters and their future! We thank them now and we will thank them tomorrow. Welcome, Reverend Harcourt. Sit down," he said animatedly, as he pointed the Reverend to the chair reserved for him.

"Thank you, kindly, Your Highness," responded Reverend Harcourt as he sat down and directed the boys to sit down beside him as well.

"Reverend Harcourt," said Oha Achinike, "I know you must be taken aback to see this many people in my compound so early in the morning. As much as you are alarmed, I am, too. It may seem unusual, however, but it is not. When matters of the magnitude of the one we now have at our hands arise, our people tend to act this way. They tend to have questions, and they tend to want answers. What you told us the other day about our two sons going to further their studies in your home country pleased all of us. It was our intention to tell the people eventually, as we told you we would do. But someone sneaked off and told the people before we told them about it and they were elated. This is why they are here in this number. However, I do not fault them. It is the habit of our people, and rightly so, when matters of this proportion arise, to be skeptical and doubtful, to have questions, and to want their questions answered. But we are as uninformed as they are about what you told us and, as such, we cannot answer most of their pressing questions. This is why we have called you. Perhaps you can shed some light that might clear up their fears and doubts."

"Thank you, Your Highness," said Reverend Harcourt. "I will be more than glad to answer their questions. But before I do that, I would want to know what you have told them already."

"Nothing, I have told then nothing, just what you told us," replied Oha Achinike.

"And do they not believe you?"

"I am sure they do."

"Then why do you need me?"

"To answer some of the questions they were asking."

"Which were?"

"Well, why not we let them ask you directly."

"Eventually we will, but I want to have an idea," responded Reverend Harcourt.

"In that case, I believe their greatest concern is: Why these boys and not the others?"

"I see," said Reverend Harcourt. "Then let us open the floor to them. I am sure some of them may have other questions, too, besides that one."

"Indeed," agreed Oha Achinike.

As this conversation was going on between the Oha and the Reverend, the people listened attentively for a chance to speak. When that chance arose, Elechi took it without being asked. He prostrated before the Oha and the council of elders and then faced Reverend Harcourt and the two boys. His eyes darted here and there as though he was nervous, and anyone who didn't know him well would think that he was. But he was not. It was his normal way of acting around people, and he was acting his normal self. Yet, everyone, including the Oha and his council of elders and even Reverend Harcourt himself, knew that his mouth was poisonous and his brain quick at skepticism and illogic. He wore his usual native *agbada or chereka nku*, which usually made him look prominent and important, even though he is more like a village wag and could care less about how he looked and what people said or thought about him.

"I have not come to make trouble, as you might assume, but to seek answers," he said, looking the Reverend intently in the eye.

"*Meka*," said Oha Achinike, as he smiled at one of his nemesis in the village.

"What I want to know first is: Why these two boys and not others?"

"Elechi," said Reverend Harcourt, "I have often found your words wise, and your skepticism refined, yet you tend to be irrational sometimes."

"How?"

"Well, why ask why these two boys?"

"Yes, why them and not the others."

"But why not them?"

"Are they not the 'weak ones'?"

"So, what if they are?"

"Simple. They should not be the ones representing our village."

"Who said anything about representing your village? Where are they representing your village?"

"Are they not the ones you have chosen to go for further studies in your home country? "Yes, they are."

"And while there, will they not be representing our village."

"Yes, they will be representing your people; they will also be representing the Waterside school."

"Then doesn't that make it reasonable to send our best and brightest."

"But, Elechi, these are your best and brightest."

"How?"

"Because they have earned their keep, and they earned it by reading every book we have in our library and by learning how to read and write within six years. They have also passed the necessary examinations for getting into a university."

"Is that right?"

"Yes, that is right," continued Reverend Harcourt. "And not only that, even though you people in this village call them the 'weak ones', we at the Waterside school call them the 'strong ones'. Better yet, we also call them the 'bright ones'."

"And why is that?"

"Because they have proven that book power is as important and relevant as physical strength, if not more. Now, when I say that they passed the examinations necessary to get into a university, it does not mean that the examinations were given to them alone. Not at all. No! The examinations were given to everyone in the senior class, and only these two boys scored the highest. In fact, they got all the answers right, and I am proud of them. And so should you and the entire village of Achinva. They have earned their keep, they have done their part, and now they need your help to get to the next level. They need help from people like you to speak and campaign so the village can sponsor their education abroad."

"And what good is in their education for the village?"

"Good question," cheered Reverend Harcourt. "This is why I often thought that you are one of the brightest brains of this village. That is a fantastic question. Now, listen. After their education abroad, these two boys will benefit your village immensely in more ways than one. In fact, I cannot even begin to name what their contributions might be, for it could be, in one word, innumerable!"

"And what will they be studying at the university?"

"This one," said Reverend Harcourt, holding Simon Wegumegu, whom the villagers knew as Ayiwe by the hand, "wants to be a doctor. That means he will come back and build a hospital and take care of every sick person in this village."

"And the other one?"

"This one here," holding Peter Amadioha, whom everyone knew as Chigozi, "wants to be a lawyer, and may even be a judge one day. Who knows?"

"Do you think they are capable?"

"Not only do I think they are capable, I know they are!"

"And when are they leaving?"

"This week."

"This week? Why? Why the rush?"

"Because their school will be opening in two weeks; they need to get prepared and to get used to the food and the weather there before school opens." This was the explanation Reverend Harcourt gave for his looming impromptu departure with the boys, but Elechi and his friends saw it differently. They were not satisfied with the Reverend's answers. They needed more explanations, which never came, for the Reverend refused to divulge more than was necessary. Besides, other people were lining up to ask their own questions, but none of their questions were as divisive and provoking as that of Elechi and his friends. After much haggling to stop Elechi's line of questioning, Oha Achinike stepped in and ended it summarily, giving others a chance to air their own views and remarks.

But Elechi would not be stopped from making his point. He would return later that day to the presence of the Oha and his council of elders to ask the remainder of his questions.

"How could it be that he waited this long to tell us if he needed our help and was not planning to steal the boys and the money?" he asked Oha Achinike and his council of elders later that day, long after Reverend Harcourt and the boys had returned to the Waterside school. But instead of arousing sympathy in the elders, Elechi's question aroused anger.

"Do you ever think positive thoughts, Nwaelechi?" asked Oha Achinike. "Ever since I have known you, you have never said anything positive, at least not to my hearing. Do good things ever come out of your mouth? Or, do we need to sacrifice a hen or a fowl to that your mouth so it can tell your brain to think good, positive thoughts instead of bad, negative ones always?"

"No, great father," said Elechi, smiling. "I do not think my mouth needs any kind of sacrifice."

"Then why doesn't it say positive things?"

"I just say what I feel, that's all."

"Now, can you begin to practice saying only what you think by trusting your brain more than your mouth?"

"But I do, great father, I think about things before I say them. Of course, I do."

"Why do you say that?"

"Because it is true."

"Did you think about what you said few minutes ago?"

"Yes, great father."

"How?"

"I am just skeptical that's all, just like every reasonable man in this village ought to be. In fact, I believe that I am more thoughtful that way than most people."

"That may be true, but most people don't talk the way you do."

"Not if they don't know what to say—, no, they don't."

"So you think you know what to say?"

"Not only that, great father, I also have something to say! And in this matter of the White man taking our children to his country to educate them, I believe that I am right to be wary about his intentions and his timing of it."

"Why?"

"I don't know; I just have that feeling."

"Well, whatever your feelings may be, hold on to them," said Oha Achinike. "What we need in this village is progress, and if that progress will come from these two boys, so be it, Nwaelechi. Do you hear me? If it will come from the White man assisting us in helping them, so be it. We will try to help them, and we will try to help the White man to help them. When they return as he had predicted they would after their studies, then we will see if they would become what the White man had predicted they would become. What you have to remember, my son, is that whatever happens in this world is not totally in our control. We human beings and every other creature on this earth are controlled externally. If a bad is going to happen, we have not the power to stop it from happening, and if a good is about to happen, we have not the power, supernatural or otherwise, to stop it from happening. We are at the mercy of *Chineke* and the gods and the ancestors. Whatever they say will be, will be. Those boys are our children, as well as their children. If they plan something good for them and they believe that the good will come by the White man taking them to his home country to educate them, who are we to stop it? And if they say that they would perish there and never come back, who are we to stop it?

"Not long ago, we in this village called these same boys the 'weak ones', but in the eyes of the White man, they are the 'strong ones'. What does that do to all the things we have known all our lives? Not long ago as well, we thought having twins was an abomination, but are not women having twins here and there in this village? Let us leave everything in the hands of the gods and our ancestors, my son. Let us let them fight our battles for us, especially the ones that we are not sure of victory. That way they will continue to support us and to come to our aid whenever we need them.

"As far as I can tell, Nwaelechi, I believe that the White man has all the good intentions. I believe that he trusts us as much as we trust him. Otherwise, what would he gain from doing us harm, an innocent people that have opened their hearts to him? What comfort would harming us and our children bring to his heart? I don't know about the rest of you, but I don't see him that way. But, of course, I am not a perfect judge of character. The human behavior is like a wind. It can blow this way, and it can blow that way. As such, I have no reason, Nwaelechi, to dampen your skepticisms completely. But reasonable and valid as they may seem, we must never let ourselves be slaves to history, lest we fall victim to future's enslavement as well. Armed with this knowledge, we must concern ourselves, therefore, with things that we can control, and the ones that we cannot control, we must learn to leave in the capable hands of the gods and our ancestors. *Nmekan!*"

Chapter 18

The Send-Off Party

The news of the sudden departure of Ayiwe and Chigozi to the White man's country loomed large in the ears of the villagers, and along with it spread rumors of what might become of them while there. Some, like Elechi and his friends, speculated that the boys would never come back to the village of Achinva after their studies. Others opined that Reverend Harcourt was merely taking them there to be enslaved. And yet a handful believed that they were going for a good cause, and that they would come back and do great things for the village of Achinva, just as Reverend Harcourt had predicted. But nothing they thought mattered anymore at this eleventh hour, for the decision had been made for them by those who held the deciding power of the village, and their decision was final.

The voice of the town crier was anything but unfamiliar and his message was anything but unexpected. The Oha and his council of elders had decided to support the two boys financially while they are abroad. By this, the village of Achinva will pay part of their school fees as well as their upkeep throughout the duration of their stay there. This kind gesture should be seen as an investment for the village, and it is not limited to these two fortunate boys, affirmed the town crier. Whoever proves him- or herself capable at the Waterside school will join them and will also be accorded the same privileges. In his message, he revealed how the funds will be generated painlessly, for it was not different from what they had been doing to support the Waterside school.

They had been doing this for a while now, to match the funding of the Waterside school. Every age group collected a certain agreed sum of money every week. The collected money was handed to the village treasurer, who then reported his total weekly collection weekly to the Oha and his council of elders. Instead of reinventing the wheel, the elders merely increased the amount by a half and the villagers obliged. For nearly a decade, paying the dues to support the school and the boys studying abroad became a routine and an aspect of the life of the people of Achinva.

Early one Saturday morning, just two days before the boys departed, the village decided to celebrate their departure. This event they called a send-off party. But Reverend Harcourt did not see any need for it. By now he knew the ways of the villagers very well and was aware of their definition of a celebration, for it was nothing short of unnecessary lavish and waste!

"Your Highness, why not save the money and give it to the boys?" he asked Oha Achinike.

"Why do you say that?" asked the old man.

"Well, I think the celebration is a waste; the money you will spend in this celebration could be better used to help the boys abroad."

"I see what you mean, Reverend Harcourt," said the old man, "and I believe that you are right. But there is one thing you must know about our people."

"What is that, Your Highness?"

"It is hard to put into words," said Oha Achinike. "Yet I must tell you one secret about our people and it is true, whether you believe it or not. You see, Reverend Harcourt, sometimes a bird does not start singing its blues until the thunder had struck with its bolts. After all, if soldier ants had not surrounded their village and imposed havoc on them, no one would have known that sheep, too, can dance well enough to make a disgruntled squirrel smile and eventually laugh out loud atop the palm tree. Now what do I mean by these sayings, you may wonder?"

"Yes, indeed, what do you mean, Your Highness?"

"You see, Reverend, naturally, we are a happy people. We are also a superstitious people. And there are skeptics among us, as you by now know. We believe in our ancestors and we believe in the gods. As I once told you, we also believe in *Chineke,* the creator! We do not do anything without consulting with them. Before we decided that it was in our best interest to support your endeavors to help our children, we had consulted with them. Although our medium affirmed that there may be a hitch along the way in the boys' success, which we have decided to ignore at this time, they approved of our decision and they are behind us totally. As far as we know, the gods are always in a celebratory mood. They are a happy bunch, and they want us to be happy also. Why? I don't know. But I tend to have an idea."

"What is it, Your Highness?" asked Reverend Harcourt.

"You see, as a leader of the people, I see the people the way I see a woman, and the gods tend to agree with me. If you are a man and you want to get to know a woman, you cannot use force. You must humble yourself and make your desire known in the most polite and logical way. Otherwise that woman will not let you touch her, especially if she is worthy of you and you of her. Managing a village such as this is like that, too. This occasion, although minute in your eyes, is huge in mine and in the eyes of the people of this village. Imagine asking common villagers to pay weekly dues out of their meager profits of selling yams and cassava and fish and other valuable farm produces. That is unheard of in this day and age. But they willingly accepted it. That is an honor to me, and to them,—and one worth celebrating! Our people say 'because it is winter, it does not necessary follow that a people must swallow their mucus: They should still be able to spit it out!'

"This is why, my friend, I want to celebrate this little success with them. This is why we celebrate any little, even insignificant progress we make. If they see it as a waste of their money and resources, they will say it before I even think about it. They are a reasonable people, and they know when a boundary is being overstepped. Now, I understand your concern for the boys. Their success means a lot to me and to this village. Yet, even when we are carrying an elephant on our heads, we do not ignore the protein a snail meat can add to our rich diet. The party, my friend, must go on!" he said and let out a loud laugh.

Reverend Harcourt could not help but join in laughing at the old man's selected words of wisdom and how he arrived at such a melodious and proverbial conclusion. Satisfied with the sermon of his host, the Reverend rose up to go while humbly excusing himself from the celebration, as it involved masquerades and ancestral homage and libations—things he had been preaching to his pupils and followers from abstaining from, as it is believed by the church to be the source of their animist bent. Yet he promised to let the boys and their mates attend the village gathering for the last time before their departure to England.

The Arena of the First Sons was packed with people of all ages. To kick-off the celebration, the Oha and his council of elders had asked the people to donate whatever they can to the boys, mainly food and livestock. These items would be sold and its proceeds will be put in the treasury for the boys. No donation was too little and none was too much. As such those who could afford it donated produce, such as yams, cassavas, plantains, bananas, coco-yams; and livestock, such as sheep, rams, goats, hens, and fowls. The yams were piled high at the center of the arena, as well as all the other items. But just minutes before the celebration peaked, they were removed and stocked away for safekeeping.

There were other dances in the village that the people could have chosen, but they chose *eregbu*. No one knew exactly why *eregbu* dance was chosen, but not many would be able to say why it should not be, for it alone produced tunes that resonated with the people of Achinva—both the living and the dead! Its melodies are memorable and scintillating to the intellect of those who know exactly what the lyrics are saying, and can interpret what the drums are telling them. One of the songs sang that day was *Otutu nzinu Chineke or Glory be to God*, and it goes like this:

Ah, Chineke, noble ancestors!
These are our children, your children!
They will soon embark on a journey
across the seas to a land far, far away.
Where they are going we do not know,
only you know,
and when they will return we do not know,
only you know.
We know we are not being deceived
because you have approved
of their journey.
We know we are not losing them to death,
which is why we are celebrating
their departure.
We beg that you and the gods guide them
as you always guide your own;
we beg that you and the gods protect them
as you always protect your own.
We ask that whichever leaf that took them there
should take them there safely,
and we ask that the same leaf return them home safely
to us.
Once this is done for us,
as it is also a homage to you, as well,
Ah, protectors and forebears,

then praise be to Chineke,
then praise will be to the gods,
and to the ancestors!

The people danced to this tune and to many others until late into the moonlit night. Had the younger ones had their way, they would have continued the celebration until the wee hours of the night. But the elders would not let them. Before he left the arena, however, Oha Achinike blessed the two boys while the villagers watched. While touching their heads as they bowed, he praised them for their achievements and urged them to continue to achieve great things for themselves and for the village of Achinva.

"All eyes are on you," he cautioned them. "You are the first; do not be the last. Our village needs you as much as you need us. As I have always said, this world is a wonderful place, and you can never know what you are going to get out of it until you try to get something out of it. As a courageous people, all we can do is try. But we can never be sure of what our effort will yield until we see the result of our efforts with our own eyes.

"Although you do not yet know what your efforts will yield," continued the old man, "all I and the entire village of Achinva can do is encourage you to try. One could be a slave today and a king tomorrow; one could be a follower today and a leader tomorrow; and one could be a 'weak one' today and a 'strong one' tomorrow. We never know these things. Only the gods know these things, and only they know them well. As for us, we are merely fishing in a vast ocean. What the catch of the day will be we do not know. Whatever you do, and wherever you go, always keep this village in the back of your mind. Remember us as we remember you. Let the leaf that took you there also return you to us. We are blessed because you are blessed, and we are thankful because you have been chosen. Your choice is not the work of man but that of the gods and the ancestors. Always remember that. We believe that they will be watching over you and that they will guide you throughout your stay and until your turn safely to us."

His speech lasted for about twenty minutes. And by the time he had completed it, the dancing and celebratory mood had fled the people. And neither the drummers nor the dancers were willing to go on. The evening ended as it began, peacefully, as the crowd dispersed one by one and in groups of four and five—and, in some cases, more. But the memory of this day never left the hearts and minds of the people of Achinva. It lingered for years, and still does, even to this day!

Chapter 19

Tidings of Despair

Several years had passed by since the two boys, Simon Wegumegu and Peter Amadioha, went to England for further studies. Except for occasional photographs and letters, the two boys were never heard from. The white missionary, Reverend Harcourt, made his yearly pilgrimage to England for his vacation, and each time he would return the parents of the boys would always pay special visits to him to inquire about their sons. "Your sons are well and healthy," he would reply. At other times, he would give them things other than photographs that the boys had given them to give whoever was in need in the village—things like used clothes and other useful items. This went on for several years. And all the while the village continued to contribute money to support the Waterside school and to support the two boys abroad. Uncharacteristically, no one complained—not even those who were known for complaining all the time—for the people really saw their weekly contribution to the Waterside school and to the boys' training in England as an investment into their future and the future of the village of Achinva.

Meanwhile, Nigeria was boiling silently inside, and a ravaging climate of change was brewing latently all over the country, irrespective of the thoughts and plans of the people of Achinva. In short, no one in the village of Achinva knew what was happening in their own country, and, frankly, as it turned out, no one cared until the water was above the neck. Instead they went about their normal business. With the exception of the pupils who attended the Waterside school and their teachers, the entire village was illiterate. They neither read the newspapers nor do they listen to the radio. In fact, they had no access to neither. Therefore knowledge of the outside world was not only a luxury but a luxury unknown to almost all of them, and those who possessed these rare luxuries, in the form of radios or newspapers, sold them to the highest bidder—that is if he or she ever found a buyer!

During the past few years since the two boys went to England, the Waterside school had graduated a few more pupils. Some of them, upon completing standard six, had gained the government scholarship and had gone to college to further their studies. Some had gone to County High Schools, some to Technical colleges, and some to Private Commercial Secondary Schools in Port Harcourt and in neighboring cities like Aba, Onitsha, Enugu. Some even went as far as Kano and Kaduna and Lagos and Abeokuta to go to school. Among these promising pupils, as Reverend Harcourt referred to them, were Silvanus Arusi, Benjamin Akirika, and Timothy Aduma. These and a few more were the best and the brightest that the Waterside school had produced within its short life, and many more were simply waiting in the wings to further their studies in England once the two boys returned, at least that was the rumor in the village at the time. To say that the optimism of the people of Achinva about their future at this period was high was to say it mildly. They howled and bragged about their achievements to their neighbors and had proof to show.

"In all fairness, however," said Reverend Harcourt during one of his conversations with visitors from other villages, "the village of Achiva is making strides, and is far ahead of the other villages in its effort to educate its children and to lay a strong foundation for its future." Things, indeed, were going well for them and the people knew it, and no one could be happier with this state of affair than their chief, Oha Achinike.

The Victims of Rivalry

"How can we do the same thing for our village?" asked Umesi Ajor, an envoy of the village of Rumuega. Mr. Ajor is educated and well-respected in his village. He is well-spoken, too, and is known for his neat dressing, as he always wore starched clothes with sharp creases that pointed at you. He is short, about four and half feet tall, and always cut his short, curly black hair low.

"What do you have in mind?" asked Reverend Harcourt.

"Well, my people want the same thing that the people of Achinva have."

"Of course, everybody wants the same thing. But can you afford it? That is the question," replied Reverend Harcourt.

"We are willing to try."

"And so are other villages."

"At what cost?"

"A lot," said Reverend Harcourt. "Look, Mr. Ajor," he continued, "I don't know what is on your mind. Even though I have an idea of why you are here, I don't know exactly what you want. But before I let you go on, I must make something clear to you. I have met with several delegates from various villages and they all want the same thing that you want. They all want me to arrange for a school to be built in their own village. I keep telling them that that will not be possible. I tell them instead that they should bring their children to Achinva, for the Waterside school is strategically positioned and large enough to accommodate everyone, but they all refuse. The reason behind their refusal, as I understand it, is because they are not friendly with the people of Achinva and, as such, cannot send their children to Achinva. The world is changing, and it is time you put all your inter-tribal and inter-village squabble behind you and work together. This is not the time and the place to segment yourselves and deprive your children of education. I see no reason why the Catholic and Baptist mission should build another school ten miles away from here. It is just not possible, so instead of asking me to build a school in your village, start looking for ways to transport your pupils to the Waterside school. Perhaps in a few years, that is, after we had grown and are ready to expand, then we can expand to your village. For now, I don't see how we can honor your request. The country is changing, the world is changing, and we don't even know what the future holds, whether or not Nigeria will survive!"

These comments from the mouth of the revered white missionary, Reverend Harcourt himself, who was known to be capable of anything, displeased Mr. Ajor. It was more of a blow to his huge ego than anything else. Nevertheless, he had nothing else to say than to say his goodbye and return to his village to relate his bad news to his eagerly anticipating but soon to be disappointed people. But just as he rose to go, the shot-wave radio broadcaster caught the attention of him and Reverend Harcourt. They held their breath and listened attentively to what the announcer had to say: *"Effective immediately, all schools, including universities in Eastern Nigeria are temporarily closed. All students and teachers must return to their respective homes and localities until further notice. Also affected in these closures are private and missionary schools throughout the affected areas. This is a special announcement from the Military Headquarters in Lagos. This is radio Nigeria, Lagos."*

The news had barely concluded when Reverend Harcourt gestured to Mr. Ajor what seemed like: I told you so.

"What are they up to now?" inquired the ill-informed man.

"I told you the country and the world are changing."

"What are you talking about?"

"Have you not been listening to the news?"

"What news?"

"About the impending war?"

"What war?"

"Then this conversation is over, Mr. Ajor," barked Reverend Harcourt to Mr. Ajor through his interpreter, Mr. Nnadiekwe. Then he walked away from his visitor and went into his backyard, still talking agitatedly. "How can someone who calls himself educated not know the current affairs of his country? What kind of education does he have? Where have knowledge and curiosity gone to? Have they gone to the market and not yet returned? What is wrong with these people? And now he is begging me to come to his village to build another school to produce more half-educated fools like him. God forbid!"

The Reverend fumed over this incident and mauled over it while listening to the radio for, perhaps, more news about what was actually happening in the world and beyond the confines of Achinva and its abounding rural villages. His shortwave radio was still on when sleep overcame him and transported him to the universe of endless impossibilities!

The village of Achinva was bustling with new faces the next day. Students were returning to their villages in droves and among them were the sons of Achinva, most of whom had graduated from the Waterside school. They scurried in one by one to their alma-mater to greet Reverend Harcourt, who was elated and happy to receive them. One of the first to show up to show his courtesy to Reverend Harcourt was Timothy Aduma, whom his teachers fondly called Mr. Adu-uma. Timothy was jet black in complexion and smiled rather easily, making his lanky frame even more adorable. His parents were not well-to-do, by the standards of the village, as was many parents in the village of Achinva. But the boy himself was a high achiever. He performed ahead of everyone in his class and always excelled with distinction in all his school activities. His classmates called him a bookworm, for he read everything and all the time.

"Look who is here," said Reverend Harcourt once he laid eyes on him. "Mr. Adu-uma!"

"Yes, sir."

"Well, aren't you looking fantastic?"

"Yes, sir, I am."

"Well, of course, it shows."

"Thank you, sir."

"Were they treating you nicely at Enugu?"

"Yes, sir, they were."

"And how were your studies?"

"Fine, sir."

"I heard the school is a very good school."

"Yes, sir, it is."

"Good to hear, good to hear," said the White man. "So you are home because of the school closures."

"Yes, sir."

"I wonder what they are up to and where all this will lead."

"I am wondering that myself, sir," said the young lad. "In fact," he continued, "I didn't like the instructions they gave us at school before we were dismissed. It made me a little nervous and unsure about my future and the future of this country."

"Why? What did they tell you?"

"They said we should join the Civilian Defense Force in our localities."

"They said that?"

"Yes, sir."

"And why does that bother you?"

"Sir, I see it as a way of recruiting future soldiers, to fight an impending war."

"Where did you get that idea from?"

"At school, sir; in fact, everyone was saying it at school. Most of us believe that war is imminent as well as inevitable. We heard it mostly from the Igbo students and we don't know what to make of it. They believe that there is a tension between the Igbos and the Hausas and the Yorubas in the military and that is the source of the tension in the country and some people are suggesting the cessation of the East from the rest of the country. And many were saying that that was why schools and universities were closed throughout the Eastern parts of the country alone. They are, therefore, urging all students to go home and join the civil defense forces in their various localities, which will make them easily accessible to military recruiters should war eventually become inevitable."

"But who will fight the war if ever there is one? Who is quarreling with who?"

"The East and the North, they said, sir."

"Over what?"

"I don't know, sir."

"I don't know either; I mean I have an idea, but I don't want to speculate."

"Then we must wait and see, sir."

"Indeed," said Reverend Harcourt, as he tried very hard to diffuse in the heart of a naïve, young man what he already knew all too well—the impending squabble among Nigerian elites, who could not find an amicable way of sharing what the British had left for them: a vacuum of power and an enormous wealth! Yet he knew that Timothy was smart enough to know Armageddon when he saw one and there was not much explaining or swaying to do. Nevertheless, the call of nature intervened and stopped the conversation from continuing, as Reverend Harcourt excused himself to the bathroom and Timothy used the hiatus to return home to meet his mother, who had not seen him and had not yet returned from farm when he returned home from school.

Chapter 20

Restless Teenagers

Teenagers was what they were, and they wanted war! Many barely knew what war was, and many had never seen or held a gun in their yet brief lifetime, yet war was in their minds and on their lips. Every morning, early, that is, they woke up the entire village with their whistling and parading exercises. They marched and sang and vowed, at least in their songs, that the atomic bomb will split before Eastern Nigeria, now Biafra, can succumb to Hausas and Yorubas rule. Their trainers shouted commands at the top of their lungs to their trainees, who, in turn, stumped their feet on the ground for attention! They harassed the villagers and flogged mercilessly whoever challenged them or accosted them or did not obey their forceful rantings. They made and broke their own laws, and they no longer heeded the laws of Achinva. From dusk to dawn the village of Achinva and its neighbors were terrorized by these restless, teenage marauders. Their leaders had guns—real guns. And even though they themselves held makeshift, wooden guns, in their minds they had power, and the power of their leaders, as they saw it, was stronger than the power of the Oha and his council of elders. In fact, in their opinion, the Oha and his council of elders had no choice but to defer to them—the Civil Defense Force, as they called themselves,—on all matters!

The Victims of Rivalry

These were merely children, pupils whose schools had closed effectively until further notice. They had no other profession and had just been given power as civil defenders according to their claim. Who gave them these powers and who and what they were defending, no one in the village of Achinva knew exactly. Some of them were by now addressed as Captain, Corporal, Sergeant, and what not. Their uniforms were not decorated with ranks, except for the ones they had added themselves, and no one in the village knew exactly how they got their uniforms and ranks. Yet the village remained arrested by this development while passionately afraid of these teenagers who had risen from among them to take full advantage of a miserable situation, and a pending war in internally fizzy Nigeria!

The teenagers were lawless and had given themselves the power to arrest, detain, and punish villagers who refused to give them food or drink or whatever it was that they needed to keep doing their duty for the government of Nigeria, as they claimed. News of war loomed as well as the fear that came with it. Who will be fighting and what they will be fighting for, no one in the village of Achinva knew. But life went on, even though un-assuredly. It was during this period of anarchy and confusion in the village and in Nigeria, that the two sons of Achinva, Dr. Simon Wegumegu and Barrister Peter Amadioha, who had traveled to England for further studies, returned home. They looked exactly as they villagers expected, healthy and full of hope. They wore suits and behaved foreign and spoke English like the White man, Reverend Harcourt. The villagers were pleased with what they saw—the yield of their investment, their hard-earned money!

Unfortunately, by the time the two men returned, Reverend Harcourt had abandoned the school and departed to England. They had met with him there. In fact, according the two men, Reverend Harcourt had encouraged them to return home. He thought that their education and knowledge might be useful in helping to solve the problem in Nigeria, and they had come to do just that: To help their motherland save itself from itself! They were full of life when they first arrived. But quickly their good humor ceased and was replaced by seriousness and rage and anger. It was not long before they clashed with the so-called Civil Defenders—marauders who had taken over the Waterside school and whose leaders now sleep in the same bed Reverend Harcourt slept. Although these high school layovers, as many of them were referred, could fool the villagers by harassing them with their meager knowledge of *un*-English English, which they used to prop up their half-educated ego, they could not fool these university graduates, and they didn't know how to deal with them either. But one thing was for sure: These well-spoken and well-educated people did not return home from England to take orders from semi-illiterates, and they made sure to keep them in their place by paying them no mind whatsoever. They went about their normal business and did things the rest of the people of Achinva could not do, especially refusing to take orders from the teenagers. But the stance of these seeming untouchables infuriated the leader of the civil defenders.

"Who do they think they are?" asked Captain Ribisi, a man of intense look, who laughed as much as a Lion played—once in a while, especially when he was not drunk! He was not from Achinva nor was he from any village known to anyone. He simply emerged from nowhere and took control of the gang of teenage marauders. He claimed to have been sent by Colonel Chukuemeka Odumegwu-Ojukwu himself to prepare the young boys for future recruitment into the Biafran army, and his followers believed him without questions. He stammered when he spoke and roared loudly even when talking to someone within an earshot. He stood about six feet tall and always wore a brown hat. And no one has ever seen him blink, at least people said so about him behind his back. He laughed only when he was drunk, or had smoked something, which was often—the drinking that is. "Bring those bastards to my office now!" he said one day to his boys. And without hesitation the teenagers rushed to fetch the two men. They met them at exactly where they thought they would be—at the palace of the Oha.

"Who wants to see us," asked the two men simultaneously.

The Victims of Rivalry

"Captain Ribisi," replied the messenger.

"What for?" inquired Barrister Peter Amadioha.

"He wants you to answer some questions about some allegations."

"What allegations?"

"We don't know, sir!"

"Tell him we are not coming; we are not his subjects."

"I don't think he will like that?" said the speaker of the group of messengers.

"Get out of my sight," screamed Barrister Amadioha. "Do you think we care about what he likes or does not like?"

Without saying anything further, the messengers departed and then, later, reported their encounter with the men to Captain Ribisi, who became suddenly infuriated. He immediately ordered his boys to arrest the two men. But it was a mistake he would never live to repeat. By tampering with these priced possessions of the village of Achinva, the civil defenders finally ran their course, for the villagers could no longer contain their anger and rage any more. They had finally crossed the line, and no one in the village of Achinva was willing to stomach their hooliganisms any longer. Men took up arms, and women rose up wildly, even more agressive than the men, to debase the "defenders." Within a day or two, the marauders were no more and their rank and file was no more. Their Captain, Ribisi, and his cohorts abandoned their posts and offices and were nowhere to be found. But this desertion of duty did not last long. Within a week another group replaced them. But these new faces were more respectful of the villagers and the Oha and his council elders. Unlike the previous group, which recruited anyone who could shout and talk loudly without making sense, these new group recruited people who could read and write and were willing to go to war if one arose. At last peace returned to Achinva, at least temporarily.

About this time, news about the worsening situation of things in Nigeria filled the airwaves and gripped the consciousness of the people, including even people who did not actually know what was happening and could care less. It suddenly became a familiar sight to see groups of men and boys surrounding their handheld shortwave radios, which they had purchased recently due to the war news, and for listening to other foreign news. Now, even though most people in the village of Achinva did not know exactly what the hoopla was all about, being illiterate and all, they had an idea that something was amiss. The two most educated men in the village, Dr. Wegumegu and Barrister Amadioha, who had just returned from England, and whom the villagers now looked up to for guidance, were working diligently to raise the consciousness of the village and to prepare them for what was inevitably coming their way. These men were believed to know what the White man knows, and they traveled back and forth to Port Harcourt. Sometimes they stayed there for over a week at a time before returning to the village on weekends, and sometimes they commuted. Rumors ran high among the villagers as to what activities they were engaged in.

Some people speculated that the men were being tapped to be the next leaders of the Nigerian nation, for their education had qualified them for such statesmanship. Others believed that the men were working hard to change the lives of everyone on the village of Achinva and beyond, and for the better! Yet, amid these speculations, no one knew quite what activities the men were engaged in or what their role in the brewing uproar in the country was, or in the pending war, will be.

One early morning, however, while the men were listening to their radio, someone shouted a cry that sent chills even to the innocent and the uninformed in the village of Achinva. The new leader of the Nigerian nation, Major General Johnson Agui-Ironsi had been assassinated. How he was killed no one knew. Why he was killed no one knew. But in the faces of the men listening to the radio, even the blind could see that Armageddon was mere minutes away!

Chapter 21

More Bad News

Until the news of the assassination of Major General Agui-Ironsi made the headlines, the majority of the people of Achinva village, most of whom were illiterates and uninformed about the world around them, did not know that his death had preceded the worst assassination plots that the young Nigerian nation had ever experienced. Previously, the leaders of country, Prime Minister Sir Abubakar Tafawa Balewa had been assassinated, the Sardona of Sokoto had been assassinated, and a whole host of others in the leadership of the Nigerian government and people. This news was just coming to the rest of the population of Achinva for the first time, and many didn't know what to make of it, and the questions they asked those who spoke English and could interpret the news to them were anything but intelligible and informed.

"Are they coming to kill all of us?" asked Oha Achinike.

"No," replied Dr. Wegumegu and Barrister Amadioha. The two men had been invited to brief the Oha and the council of elders on what they were hearing.

"Is it really true, what we are hearing about the deaths of the leaders?"

"Yes."

"Where are these things happening?"

"Lagos."
"Where is Lagos?"
"Lagos is where the leaders of Nigeria live."
"Is it far away from our village?"
"Yes, quite far away."
"Are the killers going to reach here anytime soon?"
"No, we don't think so."
"Are they at war with each other?"
"No."
"Will there be war?"
"We don't know yet."

"But who in his right mind would kill his or her own leader?" asked Oha Achinike, bluntly.

"That is the question everyone is asking," said Dr. Wegumegu.

"Have they no laws prohibiting such crime as we have here in Achinva?"

"I am sure they do. At this time we don't know the assassins' reasons for killing the people they have killed so far," said Barrister Amadioha.

"What could their reasons be?" asked Oha Achinike. "What would anyone's reason be for taking another's life? Let alone their leader? If there is a problem in the government, as their often is a disagreement between the leader and the led, why don't reasonable people sit down and talk it over and make amends where necessary to smoothen things up? Why do men resort to arms and killings at all times? Have they no sense? Even with all the book knowledge that they have, have they not learned that once blood is spilled, more blood will be spilled? I am afraid that a bigger trouble is brewing. I have a feeling that more deaths will occur and it bothers me.

"My sons," continued Oha Achinike, "this is the reason why I have called you two. I don't know a lot about what is happening beyond Achinva. I have no knowledge of the world out there, nor do I want to know. But for you two, it is different. That is why we sent you to the White man's country—to learn and to teach the rest of us. From what you have told me so far, and from what the spirits have communicated to me, I see a bigger problem ahead for this country. This is what the gods have warned me. The two of you are the pillars of this village now. You are now our eyes, our ears, and our legs outside the borders of this village. Because you have traveled across the ocean to other lands, you see far more than we see and you know about the outside world far more than we in the village know or could ever know. A storm is brewing out there, and the gods and the ancestors want me to warn you. Whatever you do, keep out of trouble. Do not put your hands on things that would tarnish your image or the image of this village. You are now our priced possessions and our pride, and all eyes are on you, and rightly so. We have invested in you; it is now your turn to invest in us. But whatever you do, be careful. We are not asking you to bring the world to us. That would be impossible. We are not asking you to change our lives overnight. That would be asking too much, and asking unreasonably, too. All we ask is that you do your best—at your own pace and with reason. That is all I have to say. That is what I have called you for."

"Thank you, great father," said Dr. Wegumegu and Barrister Amadioha almost simultaneously.

"I am just a messenger," said Oha Achinike.

"We heard what you said and we will not disappoint you or our village," said Dr. Amadioha.

"Well said, my sons."

"We will do our best and leave the rest to the gods and the ancestors," said Dr. Wegumegu.

"That is all we ask," replied Oha Achinike.

"We must leave now, great father," added Dr. Wegumegu.

"The gods and the ancestors will be watching over you as always," concluded the old man as the men prostrated and humbly exited his presence.

Every day the news got worse and worse and tension rose higher and higher. The actions of the notorious civil defenders were becoming rapacious and unbearable. Their noises were becoming louder and louder and their actions more sinister. They had no compunction whatsoever and cared less about anyone's welfare but theirs alone. They arrested and beat up anyone who did not comply with their guidelines, which was next to unruliness. As the powers of the military grew in the Nigerian nation, so did their power. They beat and tortured whomever they could lay their hands on, and they captured and raped any woman that crossed their path, married or not. It was during this air of turmoil and unrest in this part of the world that another disparaging news pierced through the radio waves.

"We are no longer Nigeria, the news said; we are now Bia-bia-ifra," stammered the interpreters, who were also learning the name for the first time.

"Bia-gini?" asked a woman, who was standing next to the people interpreting the radio announcement.

"We, the people of Eastern Nigeria are no longer part of the Nigerian nation. We are now known as Biafra, and Colonel Chikwuemeka Odumegwu-Ojukwu is our leader," repeated the radio interpreters to their bewildered and inundated audience.

"So what happens to Nigeria?" asked one man.

"Nigeria is still Nigeria, but we are no longer part of it; we are now a different country, Biafra."

"How?" asked the same man.

"Ask the radio," joked one of the interpreters.

"How did we suddenly become Biafra; what happened to Nigeria? I like Nigeria."

"We don't know," replied the interpreter. "Maybe they will tell us later. But right now we have no idea. All they are telling us is that the people of Eastern Nigerian have broken away from Nigeria and have now taken up the name, Biafra."

"What does Biafra mean?"

The Victims of Rivalry

"We don't know, just as we don't know what Nigeria means. But I am sure they will tell us very soon if we stay tuned," replied the man. And tuned they stayed, all day and all night. By now everyone was glued to his shortwave radio. News were been consumed like *gari* and soup, only unlike the later it was not digesting very well in the stomachs of its consumers. But life went on as usual, with the commanding voices and the war songs of the civil defenders getting louder and louder and hope for a better future for the people of Achinva and beyond dwindling by the minutes.

The true aftermath of the previous news of Eastern Nigeria splitting from Nigeria and becoming Biafra did not sink into most people in the village of Achinva, including even the educated ones, until months later when the news interpreters told the villagers that the Nigerian currency they now used as legal tender were now useless. Panic grew quickly among the people. Those who had much money stacked away somewhere were almost in tears and those who had no money saved at all thanked *Chineke* for making them poor at this time. But their celebration did not last long, as the same news interpreters quickly retracted their earlier news and gave back hope to the well-to-do in the village.

"The Biafran central bank will be sending loads of the Biafran currency in exchange for the Nigerian currency," reported the interpreters. But this new news would not fly. Most people still did not believe that the Biafran state was a reality; they merely dismissed it as another Igbo people's ploy or *wayo*, to cheat and to deceive! The people who thought this way were mostly the rich and the haves. They knew better than to dance to the music of the news, which was oftentimes hopeless, especially at a time as unstable as this. They stacked their money under their mattresses, in boxes, or dug a hole on their bedroom floor to hide it, and refused to buckle with the tide of change, dubbing it "a false alarm."

When the Biafran central bank's so-called loads of money finally arrived at Rumuachinva village, it was anything but a load. Only few sums of money exchanged hands. The exchange rate was bogus, way short of expectations. Ten pounds Nigerian currency was being exchanged for one pound Biafran currency, and none of the officials changing the money took the time to calculate the proper exchange rate. The Nigeria paper currency was reaped apart in the face of those who possessed them and the worthless Biafran money, which was not yet even a legal tender in most areas covering Biafra, was given in exchange. After the first wave of money changers returned home, their neighbors learned their lesson and refused to give up their hard-earned Nigerian money.

The money changers departed in frustration, for most of the villagers would not give in or give up their money despite the harassment of the soldier and the civil defenders and the money changers that they would end up destroying the money because it would in the end be useless to them. Instead of giving in and wasting their hard-earned money away, the villagers opted to take their chances.

Meanwhile the people had more to worry about than money. Their lives were in danger. News of war were looming, and the airwaves were relentless in keeping everyone informed. Names such as General Yakubu Gowon, Colonel Chukwuemeka Odumegwu-Ojukwu, "Okoko-nde", Obafemi Awolowo, Nnamdi Azikiwe, David Ejor, Chief Akintola, Hassan Katsina, M. I. Okpara, Major Nzeogwu, Emmanuel Ifeajuna, Francis Fajuyi and many more were now household names. Yet, it was no laughing matter, as war was war: brutal, even by the definition of naïve village peoples who had never laid eyes on modern, merciless war arsenals. They knew that war knows no relatives, and can pit brother against brother and sister against sister. By now, however, the villagers knew who was fighting the war: Biafra was fighting Nigeria. Why they were fighting and when the fighting will begin was, however, anyone's guess. But it was not happy times—the mere thought of war!

Chapter 22

Rumors of War

As it became imminent that war was inevitable, the activities of the so-called Civilian Defense Forces escalated. For some unexplained reason, they became more brutal and heinous than ever before. They raped women with recklessness and beat up any man who spoke his mind against their unprecedented atrocities. They were not respected by the villagers; there was no reason to respect them due to their ill-deeds. But they demanded respect and got it however they can, thus sending chills and fears to the heart of a people who had done nothing to deserve disrespect and disregard. With this change of attitude came a change of name within a fortnight. They were now known as the Biafran Militia Forces. And they cemented this name and their newly acquired attitude with songs such as:

Biafra! Biafra!
We are going to win the war.
We are the Biafran Militia Forces....
We will never rest,
not even for a second,
until the war is won.
We will never give in,
not even for a day,

*until the last blood is dropped
for our freedom
and self rule!*

A host of other things changed in their behavior, too. They now wore full military uniforms, and their senior members carried guns and wore pistols on their belt. Their newly hired recruits and those who were at the bottom of the ranks carried wooden guns still. The later, rather than the former, were the ones tormenting the villagers the most. Although their wooden guns had no bullets in them and could not fire or kill, the villagers feared them nonetheless, for they did not know that the guns were mere wood and had no bullets in them. Whether possessing this knowledge would have made any difference in the villager's psyche is anyone's guess. In hindsight, however, most of them, when asked, wished they had known this fact all along. But then the hypocrites would have found another way of imposing fear on their innocent victims, someone argued.

The tune of the radio changed, too, during this hostile period. Instead of Radio Nigeria, Lagos, listeners heard Radio Biafra, Umuahia. The news was now read in English and in the Igbo language. It was at this point that the people of Achinva knew that war was at their door steps. The news have come home at last. Illiterates who waited for the news, which was being read in English to be interpreted for them into local Ikwerre language, could now listen to the news for themselves. The news was now read in the Igbo language, which almost everyone in Achinva could speak and understand.

With this newly acquired medium, the proponents of the state of Biafra took their case to the people of the interior Eastern and Southern Nigeria. More and more frightening and enticing songs could be heard in the radio. Most notably was a song which sounded thus:

*We are Biafrans forever!
We are an independent people
in an independent nation,*

The Victims of Rivalry

and we are independent minded.
We want our freedom,
and we want it now!
We want neither the White man
nor the Hausa man
nor the Yoruba man
to rule us.
We want neither the green man
nor the yellow man to rule us.
Instead of the white man
or the Hausa man
or the Yoruba man
   to rule us,
the atomic bomb will blow up
into pieces
in this land of Africa!

Now, to the villagers, this song made no sense. But to the educated people among them, it did. "How did Biafra acquire the atomic bomb?" they asked one another.

"Who told you they had an atomic bomb?" asked Dr. Wegumegu, along with Barrister Amadioha, both of whom suddenly joined a crowd of young, educated youngsters listening to the radio.

"We heard it on the radio," replied one of the boys.

"And you believe them?"

"Why not?"

"You think atomic bomb is acquired by mixing *gari* and soup?" This comment brought laughter to a rather somber audience. "No, I don't think so," said the young man, "but that is the claim they are making in the radio."

"That they have atomic bomb?"

"Yes."

"Don't believe everything you hear in the radio," advised Dr. Wegumegu. "Most of the things you will hear on this radio from here onwards are propagandas—they are not true! They are just claims to scare the opponent."

"Why do they use propaganda?" asked the young man.

"Oh, you wouldn't understand; it is another kind of warfare."

"And why would they be talking about atomic bomb if they don't have it."

"To put fear into people like you and me."

"And for what purpose?"

"Again, you wouldn't understand: it is to gain psychological advantage over their opponent. Let me give you an example," said Dr. Wegumegu to an eager audience of educated and half-educated young men. "Using propaganda to scare your opponent during wartime is like carrying a gun without a bullet."

"How?" inquired another man curiously.

"Because people are always afraid of a gun, whether the gun is loaded or not; the fact that it is a gun, is shaped like a gun, which has the capacity to kill, commands respect. A good propaganda can scare your opponents and make them do things they otherwise would not normally do."

This conversation went on for a while. But as it was beginning to tail off, a group of armed Biafran Militia Forces stormed the village of Achinva. They had come with more Biafran currency and wanted the people to change all their money. The new government of Biafra does not want to see the Nigerian currency any longer, as it was no longer a legal tender, they claimed. Whoever possessed the Nigerian money was considered a saboteur and must be dealt with severely or summarily. Without wasting time, they took their case to Oha Achinike and instructed him to send the town crier to announce to the village that the soldiers and the Militia Forces will be searching every house and every nukes and crannies of the village of Achinva for hidden or hoarded Nigerian currency.

Throughout that day the Arena of the First Sons was filled to capacity, as the overwhelmed villagers poured in to exchange the Nigerian money for the Biafran one. As before, some were given exactly what they brought in, but most were cheated out of their hard-earned money. Those who refused this kind of injustice and protested were severely beaten and denied their entire money altogether.

At the end of the day the Biafran objective in the village of Achinva was achieved at the expense of a subdued, angry, frustrated, and powerless villagers, whose daily lives hung on an impending war—a war most people now believe to be between the Igbos and the Hausas and the Yorubas, the Christians and the Muslims, the so-called Biafrans and the so-called Nigerians: a hopeless, meaningless civil war, they called it. A war that was nothing more than a plot by the educated and the haves to destroy the lives of the poor and the have-nots of both parties, who, in actuality, would be the ones fighting and dying needlessly for it!

Chapter 23

War!

It was a normal day, a day like any other in the village of Rumuachinva. It had rained torrentially the previous day, and so the blue sky was clear and bright. The sun rose and shone like it normally does, pointing its rays sharply on southern Nigeria. European bombs, *ogbunigwe*, and mortar shells could be heard from the distance as had been the case in the previous months and years. In short, the people of Achinva expected no war escalating beyond the familiar misery associated with squabbling African tribes, and nothing out of the ordinary was heard in the news to suggest otherwise. Suddenly, however, the sound of bombs and mortar shells, which for the previous months and even years had been heard from afar, began to be heard closer and closer. No one knew what to make of the new development, but it was not long before the people began to feel and to believe that something ominous was in the offing. "Was this another form of propaganda?" "Has the war finally arrived?" These were some of the questions the villagers were asking one another. But the Biafran radio broadcasters assured everyone that nothing was amiss, and that people should go about their normal business and mind less about the impending war, for it was a day like any other. But no one who possessed the ability to reason for him- or herself believed the babble of "*Okoko-nde*"—the

The Victims of Rivalry

Biafran propaganda machine! Even though everything he said were being countered word for word by Radio Nigeria, Lagos, for some inexplicable reason most people, especially the illiterates, believed him and, as such, saw or felt no pressure of war coming their way and destabilizing their lives. After all, the radio announcer was one of them and was speaking a language they can hear and understand—the *Igbo* language!

However, while this state of uneasiness and the anticipation of a doomsday held some people captive, news came that a rocket whose source was unknown had struck the lone *iroko* tree at the center of the Achinva village market. The rocket, it was rumored, was intended to wipe out the entire village of Achinva, but the gods intervened, it was believed, and the rocket struck the *iroko* tree instead, killing it instantly by breaking it in half.

But why target Achinva village? That was the question no one was able to answer. Yet tension and suspicion about what was happening rose high, and the hopelessness of the people rose even higher. However, even as these questions and concerns loomed in people's mind, many were not in the mood to linger and be caught unawares by the coming war. People scrambled helter-skelter, packing their belongings, seeking shelter, and hiding wherever they felt safe and protected, even while aware that there was no hiding place from bombs and mortar shells whose minds had been made up to fall wherever they may by those who were, perhaps, shooting them aimlessly from afar.

The war finally reached Rumuachinva, full-blown, a few days later. During this time of worry, Wori, a boy of about six or seven years old at the time clung to his mother in fear. He went everywhere his mother went and held on tightly to the edge of her lapper, crying for his mother's attention—a thing that the impending war had deprived him of late. At this point men with blood splattered all over their face could be seen fleeing and running for their lives, and overwhelmed women and men could be heard desperately screaming and calling on their children to calm down and to heed their biddings as they prepared to pack up and run. This was when Wori's father, Uchegulem Vemehuru, told Wori's mother and his other wives to pack their few belongings and seek a hideout immediately.

"Where should we go?" asked Nyemachi, Wori's mother.

"I don't know—anywhere—the farm! The bush! The forest! Anywhere but here! Take the children with you and go anywhere and hide!" shouted Uchegbulem.

"But there is not hiding place for bombs and mortar shells."

"I know."

"So why are you telling us to go somewhere and hide."

"Woman, shut up your mouth and do what you are told! This is not the time to quarrel or argue with me. Get going, will you?" This was the last time Wori heard from his father. Moments after this exchange, his mother, Nyemachi and her co-wives packed up a few of their belongings, loaded it on their heads and shoulders and departed to the swampy, thick bushes and forests that surrounded Achinva village.

Nyemachi had four children—one girl and three boys. The girl, Everechi, who was also the oldest, was about four feet tall at the time. She smiled often and was always in good spirits. Her younger brother, Kinika, was about ten years old and seemed to be more concerned about the war than her elder sister, for he wore seriousness all over his face. Wori and his younger brother, Uche, came third and last, with Uche only a year or two younger. It was, indeed, a tight-knit family, with their father at the head. But the war changed everything. When the war broke and they had to run for their lives, their mother, Nyemachi, told her only daughter to pack a few of her clothes and her other priced belongings. She also told Uche to do the same. Her co-wives did the same for their children, too, and quickly the journey to everywhere and nowhere without their husband and father began.

The Victims of Rivalry

The path leading to Asumini the main farmland of the people of Achinva was crammed with people vying to escape the encroaching war. But nowhere was safe, and they knew it. Bombs and mortar shells were falling indiscriminately to a point where a whole family or even a whole village could be wiped out in a hurry. But Nyemachi and her children and her co-wives did not mind. They kept on running. At one point, however, the chaos grew tenser and the group had to split up. The saying "war knows no relatives" became real for this once happy family. Everyone and every group were on their own as they struggled through the forest brush to escape a war that had finally reached their homestead.

"Where are we going?" Wori finally asked his mother after he and his brothers and sister had walked for nearly a whole day alongside their mother, while holding on tightly to her hand.

"Hush," said Nyemachi, "I will tell you later." But the later never came. They had trekked all day inside the narrow bush paths and had neither rested nor eaten anything. No one was more aware of this fact—the fact they needed to eat—than Wori, whose stomach had since lost patience and could not stop complaining. And so from time to time he would remind his mother with the words:

"Mama, I am hungry."

"Me, too," Nyemachi would reply.

"So can we stop and eat?"

"Yes, very soon."

"How about here?"

"Yes, Wori, we will stop very soon."

"How about now?"

"Yes, Wori, very soon."

The boy continued asking these nagging questions and his mother kept giving him the same reply. And even though this boy-mother exchange was amusing, no one running with them was in the mood for laughter. The war was not a laughing matter, and neither was running from it. By now the group, which had been joined by other unknown faces, became quite multitudinous. They were no longer walking in the familiar farm paths and terrains but were making new ones with their machetes and legs and bare hands. They kept walking until it was well into the night. They stopped walking when they were deep into the forest and felt somewhat safe from the marauding and hungry Biafran soldiers, who were also running for their dear lives from the encroaching, well-equipped Nigerian soldiers. Yet, no one—not the soldiers and not the villagers—were safe from the indiscriminate bombs and mortar shells that fell near and far and often. Nevertheless, they were content with their dreamlike hiding. At this point they rested, ate, and slept, amid the random, intermittent gunfire, until the next day.

Throughout the night the war raged on. Gunshot sounds were everywhere, as well as bombs and mortar shells. Sleep was the last thing anyone thought about, especially the adults. Some of the children slept soundly, and some cried all night long, enraging their already enraged mothers even more! Food was scarce, but Nyemachi and her co-refugees managed with what they had, which was not much. Although the people had known for months, and even years, that the war was inevitable, no one actually prepared for it in the form of putting food aside for war time. Until that time, they had never known a war where an entire village would have to pack up and leave their homes. It had never happened.

"Who prepares for war but one who makes trouble," said Elechi, who, along with his wife and children, had joined Nyemachi and her children in the forest. The two families had met accidentally and decided to stay together.

"Where is Uchegbulem, your husband?" Elechi had asked Nyemachi the moment he saw her.

"I don't know."

"What do you mean by 'you don't know'?"

The Victims of Rivalry

"Well, it is true, I don't know," said Nyemachi. "He told us to protect ourselves and that he will take care of himself while protecting our properties at home."

"You mean he did not run away."

"No, he did not."

"Are you serious?"

"Yes, I am; he said he was man enough to face death and he was not letting foreigners take over his compound and properties. Not in this life; not ever!"

"So you mean he is at home now?"

"I am sure he is," replied Nyemachi. "He was there when we left. Whether he is still alive or not is another question. I told him to come with us but he would not hear it."

"Well, that is his choice," said Elechi. "As long as he made the decision and it was not imposed on him, I support him. However, I would not elect to be in his shoes."

"Why?"

"My family is why. I cannot afford to take my eyes off my wife and children: I will die where they die and I will live where they live. Yet, I can understand the decision of men like your husband to protect the homestead. As such, I don't blame him at all. We are a peace-loving people. We did not cause this war. We didn't ask for this war. We had nothing to do with it, and yet here we are running, running from our homes and paying for the greed and misery of others." Elechi, known for his talkative tongue, ranted and ranted about the war and the *wayo* men of Hausa and Youruba and *Isoma*, whose greed and insatiable appetite for fame and wealth had brought misery to him and his beloved Achinva. Nyemachi had since stopped talking, and there was no one else to join in his conversation, so he spoke to himself for a while and then stopped. As soon as he stopped talking, a roar of gunfire exploded near them. This was followed by a loud noise that sounded like a bomb and then another and then another—. And then, suddenly, while the bewildered and frightened group watched, a mortar shell exploded a few feet away from where they were hiding, which was deep in the forest.

"So the bomb also found us here," said Elechi.

"It looks like it," responded Nyemachi.

"Then we must move."

"Move to where?"

"Anywhere but here," replied Elechi. "We cannot stay here. The next one may fall on us. Everyone, pack your things, we must move quickly." With these final words, Elechi prevailed and the group moved. It was their third day of running and sleeping in the forest. Food had run very low, and exhaustion had set in. Those who carried large boxes of their belongings no longer had the required energy to bear the load on their heads or shoulders. Yet they did not want to abandon their only prized possessions in the middle of nowhere. This was when Elechi suggested that they open their luggage and take out only things they would need, things that would keep them alive in the forest, and then hide or abandon the rest. The suggestion made sense, and the group stripped themselves of the unnecessary load and continued on with their hapless journey.

Nyemachi made sure that all her children were tagging along. To reassure herself, she had a quick roll call:

"Everechi."

"Maa."

"Kinika."

"Maa."

"Wori."

"Maa." She did not have to call Uche, for he was fastened tightly in her back with lapper and was deep asleep. It was a critical moment of their journey, and she wanted to make sure that all her children were with her.

In front of the refugees appeared suddenly a fast-moving stream, and to continue on with their journey, they must cross this water. It was, indeed, a dangerous task but one that they must engage in if they wish to keep moving. The bombs were falling randomly now, and gunfire was piercing the dark sky like firecrackers, and they were on the run for their dear lives. Ahead of them was a family whose father, like theirs, was missing. The mother had about ten children with her, most of whom were young and helpless. The older ones helped with their siblings, yet a few remained that no one could care for or hold by the hand as they crossed the raging, fast-flowing stream.

The teary mother pleaded with her children to brave the situation, but some hesitated. The guns and the bombs were raining down faster than ever and troupes and troupes of people wanted to escape by crossing this stream before they became the victim of this most unfortunate of rivalry. Due to the pressure of others who were following from behind them, the overwhelmed mother abandoned two of her children and moved on with the ones who could brave the storm. But one of them, a girl, would not let her. She cried and clung on to her mother, whose two hands were tied up literally, for she had one child tied in her back, held two by the hand, and carried a huge load of all her family possessions in her head and without support.

The little girl clung to her mother until they reached the middle of the stream. Yet, she held on tightly to the tail of her mother's lapper, all the while crying. Suddenly, however, the lapper in her mother's waist gave way, for the girl had unknowingly loosened it, and so both the lapper and the girl were carried away like debris in a flowing river. She cried and cried, but no one had the stamina to retrieve her from the fast-moving current. Meanwhile her little brother, who was afraid of water and could not cling to their mother, stayed ashore and wailed and cried for his mother to come back for him. He was abandoned. The refugees did not look back, and neither did his mother, and, to this day, no one knew exactly what had happened to either this boy or his sister.

Chapter 24

War Over!

At about the tenth day since the actual war began, news reached the people who had been hiding in the abounding forests and bushes that the war was over. Yet, skirts of gunfire and mortar shells and bombs could still be heard from far, and sometimes even near. The refugees were skeptical of this sudden announcement of the end of the war. They did not believe anyone and so they continued to hideout in the bushes. It took the town crier and a few of the brave men of Achinva who stood their grounds at home throughout the war to go into the bushes and forests to announce that the war was finally over and that it was okay to return home.

"*Orgu vielae! Orgu vielae!*" they shouted. And this announcement was followed before and after by the sound of the metal gong, which the town crier used to alert the people. It was during this period that the refugees began to believe that it was actually safe to return home.

The town crier boomed the metal gong in the middle of the forests, and then followed it by the announcement:

"*Nnewe Oha ka mekanu anu ka nu orgu viele.*

Nnovula nya oro orgu viele."

Upon hearing the call for everyone to return to a safe home by their Oha, the refugees trooped back home one by one. Most were

The Victims of Rivalry

emaciated, and some looked haggard as would anyone who had not eaten food or drank a clean cup of water for nearly two weeks and counting! It was a thing to behold to believe! An eyesore, indeed, it was. Mothers and fathers clung to the bones of their dying children, as well as their elderly parents and relatives. They did not know whether to cry or to laugh. On the one hand they want to celebrate, for they were happy that they had survived the war, and that the war was over, but, on the other hand, their situation was not a laughing matter. Most were seriously sick, and at the brink of death. Yet, they would take life anytime if given a choice between living and dying, for one living still had hope, and hope was all they had as they returned home to count their blessings and to see what was left of their homes and properties.

To many, unfortunately, nothing much was left. The Biafran soldiers, who were being pursued by the Nigeria soldiers first reached the village of Achinva and, with their voracious appetite, after having being starved for days while on the run, ate whatever they could lay their hands on. They broke down doors and entered houses with impunity and took whatever food was in the house. They killed goats, chickens, fowls, dogs, cats, and sheep. They uprooted coco-yams in the farms and in the gardens, cut down plantains and bananas. They also cut down coconut trees and uprooted cassava tubers. These things they did without remorse, and who can blame them. After all, they were hungry and had been starving for days, if not months. But they had only few days to do their damage to Achinva, for the Nigerian army were on their trails.

Soon, however, the village of Achinva was engulfed by the Nigerian army as well. They, too, were hungry, but not as starved as the Biafran soldiers and not as emaciated and desperately needing. They looked healthy and carried guns and huge quantities of ammunitions, as opposed to the Biafran soldiers who merely carried machetes and, sometimes, what looked like a two by four wooden logs. Some of the Nigerian soldiers wrapped bullets around their necks and bodies and fired their guns into the air without restraint. The difference between them and the Biafran soldier was without question. They waved the Nigerian flag and shouted "One Nigeria! One Nigeria!" and forced the returning, starving refugees to repeat the words after them. Whoever hesitated or refused to say these words were beaten mercilessly with the head of the gun or shot at point blank range while his family and relatives watched.

From time to time a group of celebrating Nigerian soldiers could be seen singing songs such as:

Ojukwu wanted to scarter Nigeria,
but Gowan said Nigeria must be one.
We are working together with Gowan
to keep Nigeria one.
One Nigeria! One Nigeria! One Nigeria!
Oshaygbey! Oshaygbey! Oshaygbey!
Hip! Hip! Hurrah!
Hip! Hip! Hurrah!

Indeed, the Nigerian soldiers were happy, or so they the seemed, and they wanted the people of Achinva to join in their happiness, but the people were not in the mood for a celebration. These soldiers behaved as though God had given them the key to life, and so they danced, as if it was one of their *fatigue duties*, and forced the villagers to dance with them, too. But the people were hesitant and reluctant. Yet the soldiers were adamant and would have none of it. They forced the people to queue up and dance and praise Nigeria and loud her victory over Biafra. While some people yielded to this forced celebration, others bluntly refused. They had more to worry about than to sing and dance because someone wanted them to. But those who refused the soldiers' order to dance were summarily executed before the watchful eyes of their families and children.

One of the first to pay a price of death for refusing to dance was Uchebulem Vemehuru, the husband of Nyemachi. He had just come out of his hiding in his compound and was searching for his family's whereabouts among the returning refugees when a soldier called him out to dance.

The Victims of Rivalry

"I am not in the mood to dance," he said bluntly, according to eyewitness.

"Why?" the soldier replied.

"I am looking for my family; I'm afraid that they are dead."

"So what if they are dead? What are you going to do about it? After all we are at war."

"Well, I want to find out first if they are alive."

"No, you must dance first," insisted the soldier.

"But I don't want to."

"You have no choice, old man; we are celebrating Nigeria's victory and you must dance with us!"

"But I don't feel like dancing; I am looking for my family!" he shouted back at him.

"Either you dance now or I'll kill you," the soldier threatened.

"Then go right ahead and kill me," Uchegbulem murmured under his breath, but the soldier heard him. Without waiting for further altercation, the soldier opened fire and Uchegbulem fell to the ground and died instantly. A makeshift grave was ordered dug near where a multitude of refugees gathered, and he was buried quickly before any of his family could find him.

In the meantime, Nyemachi and her children were on their way home. They headed for the same place where Uchegbulem had been shot to death not long ago. In fact, she had no idea that her husband and father of her children had been killed senselessly, and no one told her. Along with other families who were also returning home, they were about half a mile away from Achinva when they saw about one hundred corpses laying on the ground. These were non-uniformed Biafran soldiers who were overrun by the Nigerian soldiers. The sight of it overwhelmed the children, most of whom had never seen a dead body before.

It was late in the evening, and daylight was slowly making room for nightfall. Corpses were laying on both sides of the narrow, main farm road leading into Rumuachinva village, leaving only a tiny trail for passersby. It was during this tedious walk home that Everechi, the only daughter of Nyemachi, unknowingly stepped on one of the corpses scattered all over the place. At first she did not know what she had stepped on. But when she looked and saw that she had inadvertently stepped on a corpse, she cried and wailed and never stopped sobbing about it for days on end. And to make matters worse, Uche, his brother could not stop teasing her about it long after the war had ended. He reminded her of it whenever they disagreed and whenever he wanted to edge her out in an argument. To Everechi, however, even to this day, this incident and the knowledge of her father's death became a memory of the war that could not be erased. From that day, she, too,—as she later acknowledged, and like the village of Achinva— became the target victim of this sibling rivalry.

Chapter 25

Parade of the Refugees

The trek home for a people who had become refugees in their own village was arduous and painful. The Rumuachinva main farm road was packed with desperate people who wanted to get home to reunite with their displaced children, fathers, mothers, and relatives. In the heat of the war, no one knew where anyone was and no one could do anything about it even though they cared deeply for one another. But now that the war was over, or seemed to be over, and the dust was about to clear, and care and compassion were beginning to return to the people's consciousness, mothers were looking for children, husbands were looking for wives, and relatives were searching the whereabouts of one another. Nigerian soldiers and some of the brave men and woman of Achinva who braved the war and never ventured to run to anywhere were all over the place searching and reuniting people. It was chaotic, to say the least. Gun shots and sounds of random bombs and mortar shells could still be heard, but they were from afar. It was as though the peeling and ravaging of the soldiers had passed over Achinva village like an influenza and had moved on to neighboring villages and it was Achinva's time to pick up itself, dust up itself, and hope that the hapless war does not return!

However, some soldiers lingered while others continued on to the warfront. Why these ones stayed behind, no one knew. But speculation abounded. Some surmised that they stayed behind to hold the conquered territories and to prevent the Biafran soldiers from retaking it. Others, and, indeed, the majority of the people, thought that the remaining soldiers were thieves who had abandoned their duties and instead focused their attention on rapping women and on taking advantage of the people of Achinva.

The palace of the Oha, where the villagers felt somewhat safe, was packed with refugees, for the Oha was guarded by the bravest men and women that Achinva could afford. These refugees did not want to go home, for they still feared for their lives. The palace of the Oha was protected by the village sharpshooters and snipers, who were hiding at all the strategic corners of the compound, mainly atop trees, and who had been ordered to shoot at sight any soldier or foreigner who ventured into the palace of the Oha with the intent to harass or torment him.

Most of the people seeking refuge at the place of the Oha were women and their children, and almost all of them were encouraged to do so by their husbands. A credible rumor was spreading that the Nigerian soldiers, the ones who still lingered around, were indiscriminately capturing women and gang-rapping them, and it did not matter whether the women were married or not. Young girls, most of whom were underage and virgin, were their target and were there for the taking. It was painful for the villagers to watch, especially since they could do nothing about it. But the soldiers didn't care. It was not unusual, at the time, to see a young girl who could not walk well because the soldiers had ravaged her beyond mending. And all these were done to the girls and to the woman at the watchful eyes of their helpless fathers and mothers and relatives and husbands. It was a lost cause, many thought. The soldiers were next to the gods, the untouchables. They had guns and they had power; the villagers had fear and nothing more!

When the soldiers noticed the multitude of people camped at the place of the Oha, they took action. They gave orders and

The Victims of Rivalry

forcefully moved the reluctant crowd to a large open field, where the sun baked and roasted their skin until it was almost edible. The people looked haggard and hungry, yet pity was the last thing in the hearts of these Nigerian soldiers. They whipped everyone to order and horded them like cattle to the place where they wanted them to stay before they could safely return to their homes or what was left of their homes. It was during this parade of the refugees that a young soldier spotted Everechi, the lone daughter of Nyemachi and the fallen Uchegbulem.

"Come here!" the soldier ordered. But she would not oblige. "I say come here now!"

"Who? Me?" the young girl, who was seventeen at the time, managed to say, pointing at herself while shivering.

"Yes, you, come here!" the soldier ordered. Shaking uncontrollably at this point, the shy, confused girl, who was still holding on to her sobbing mother, stepped slowly to where the soldier stood. He put his arms around her and proceeded to take her to the soldier's makeshift quarters, which was Uchegbulem's, Everechi's father's compound.

"What is your name?"

"Everechi."

"Are you afraid?"

"Yes."

"Nothing to be afraid of; just come with me," said the soldier. But the confused girl was reluctant. She looked at her mother or where she thought her mother sat, but her mother was no longer there. Nyemachi's motherly instinct would not let her sit there and watch her only daughter, who was still a virgin and was still being courted by potential husbands, to be used and spoiled by a soldier who did not intend to marry her. While the soldier was still questioning her daughter, she abandoned everything, including her other children, and ran straight to the palace of the Oha to report her plight.

"My daughter, my only daughter had been taken by a soldier," she cried and fell on the ground in the face of the Oha and his council of elders. Without asking much questions, the Oha sent people to intervene and bring the young girl to his palace.

"Tell the soldiers that that young lady is my proposed future wife, and that I have already paid part of the bride price," he told the messengers. The messengers arrived just in time and told the soldier what the Oha had told them. Fearful of what might happen to him or rather what his superiors, who respected the Oha and the village people, would do to him if he did not comply and release the girl, the young soldier gave her up. His fear was not unfounded however, for the General commanding their battalion, whose nickname was "The Bible", was, at the time, residing inside the palace of the Oha, and he was known to summarily execute any soldier who disrespected the Oha or the villagers, especially if it was brought to his attention. Whatever wrong that was done to the village or anyone living in it was done in his absence or behind his back. He was, no doubt, a peace maker. He was also a no nonsense kind of person, and without him around no one knew what would have become of the people of Achinva and their belonging, for he brought with him order, rationality, fairness, and stability. Why he, too, lingered around after his fighting forces were long gone, no one knew. But most people were glad he stayed and prayed that he alone and not his soldiers should be allowed to stay.

After this incident, Everechi never left the palace of the Oha until the war had ended and the soldiers were all gone. She was given a room and treated like one of the many wives of the Oha. Her mother and siblings and relatives went to visit her from time to time. Sometimes they brought her food, the little they could afford, even though they didn't need to. Above all, Everechi was lucky. She was one of the few young, mature women in the village of Achinva whom the Biafran/Nigerian war did not take their virginity by force!

But the entire village of Achinva was not so lucky. During this parade of the refugees, the soldiers maimed and slaughtered

The Victims of Rivalry

whoever did not obey their orders, including dogs and cats and goats. They simply brought them aside and shot them while the people watched. One of these incidents occurred during what the soldiers called "Operation Counterfeit." They brought plenty of firewood and made a bonfire of sort in the middle of the crowd and the operation began.

"If you have in your possession the Biafran currency, consider it a counterfeit and toss it into the fire," they shouted.

"Are we exchanging them?" asked someone bravely.

"No," said one soldier.

"Then what do we get in return for burning our money?"

"Nothing."

"Nothing?"

"Yes, nothing," repeated the soldier. "The Biafran money is no longer a legal tender in Nigeria. If you have any of that ugly money, throw it into that burning fire. The Biafran money must burn in hell fire!" he shouted.

"But what if we decide to keep it," asked the same man.

"For what?" questioned the same soldier.

"As a souvenir."

"No!" shouted the tall, dark Hausa soldier, whose tribal marks were vicious and astoundingly visible. "Put all your Biafran money in the fire now!" he repeated. "If you do not have them here and you know where they are in your home, go now and bring them here. Otherwise if we find them on you after today, you will be killed instantly and your money will be burned. This is an order," he concluded. And truly an order it was. One by one the villagers emptied the only form of currency and purchasing power they had in the world (which, for some, were their only meaningful possession) into the open blaze and watched them being consumed. If you said you did not have any money, you were beaten until you said the truth, and if you are not lucky, you were either beaten or shot to death during interrogation.

While the search for money was going on, the soldiers captured Dr. Simon Wegumegu and Barrister Peter Amadioha, the two most educated sons of Achinva. Anyone could see that the semi-illiterate soldiers were intimidated by the way these highly educated men carried themselves. Even the clothes these men wore did not show the distress of a war time. They were shaven clean and were well-dressed, and their demeanor gave them away as the pride of the village of Achinva. Amid the parade, they were brought to the center of the crowd, near where the fire was burning, and told to sit on the ground. All the while, however, they were being beaten and slapped around as though they were thieves. Hesitantly, the two obeyed and sat on the ground. They were then told to remove their coats and they did. The fearful villagers didn't know what to make of this development; most knew without a doubt that these two could easily be casualties to this war, judging from the way things were turning out. As one group of soldiers were giving them these orders, another group were busy reading some papers and notes they had found in the twain's pockets and houses.

Within minutes, the two groups of soldiers converged and began questioning the men. After several minutes, they were joined by their commanding General, "The Bible." He, too, began to query the men after he read the paper that was handed to him. But by now the men had become taciturn. They had made up their mind to not speak or divulge anything that will make matters worse for them. But it was too late, for the soldiers had already reached a decision on what they wanted to do to them. Yet "The Bible" would not give them the order. He wanted to make sure that he was doing the right thing, so he went to query the men again.

"Who gave you these documents?" he asked them.

"Are they not official government documents?" replied Dr. Wegumegu.

"Why are you answering my question with a question?"

"I didn't mean to, sir."

"I bet you didn't," said The Bible. "Now, tell me, the two of you, how did you come to possess a paper like this?

"It was given to us," replied Barrister Amadioha.

"By who?"

The Victims of Rivalry

"By the government."

"Which government?"

"The one whose name appears there."

"I see, but I want to hear it from you," said The Bible. "Which government are you referring to?"

"The Biafran government."

"Are you two Biafran government officials?"

"No."

"But these are appointment letters."

"Yes, but we have not been posted anywhere yet."

"But you would have been posted if Biafra had won the war, right?"

"We don't know, sir."

"What do you mean?"

"Just what I said, sir, we don't know."

"Were you praying for Biafra to win?"

"No."

"Were you cheering for Biafra?"

"No."

"Are you an ally of Biafra?"

"No."

"Then why do you have in your possession an appointment letter from the Biafran government promising you a permanent secretary position after the war had ended and Biafra is victorious?" The men did not answer. "You two were going to become big, rich men after the war ended, and you were just buying your time, right?" The men did not reply. "Well, I have news for you," said The Bible. "All that dreams of yours will become history. All friends of Biafra are my enemy. At this moment, you two are my enemy and no amount of pleading will keep you alive." With these final words, he ordered his men to kill them both. Fearing that he might change his mind, as he often does, for he is a compassionate man, the soldiers stripped the men of their clothings and paraded them naked at the watchful eyes of the sobbing villagers. The women in the crowd turned their faces in disgust. The soldiers spat at the men, lavished insults on them, and slapped their faces until they were swollen and splattered with blood. They then told them to lay face-up on the bare ground. Then with what looked like a table knife, they disemboweled them both and exposed their intestines while they were still alive. Crying loudly and struggling to stay alive, the men took their last breath and died instantly atop their own pool of blood. The villagers could not believe it. It was like a dream. And it was as if they were witnessing their property being stolen or their investment being lost to an unstable market.

When news reached the Oha and his council elders that the soldiers had taken the lives of the most prized possession of the village of Achinva, they cried and wailed. They sent for The Bible, demanding some explanation, but he would not honor their request. He would not even venture to be in their presence. It was no use, however; the deed was already done, and there was nothing anyone could do to change it. And so, in a meaningless war that should never have been fought in the first place, the greatest losers were the innocent people of Rumuachinva, and they knew it. Their loss was heavy and unforgiven, as many of them would later say, and its ill-effects still lingers to this day. Although they had made substantial headway ever since the war ended, recovery had been slow. They had, however, never since stopped mourning their loss and wondering what would have become of Achinva if—!

Chapter 26

The Windfall of the War

One by one the people of Rumuachinva returned to their village and to their rummaged, ravished homes to find nothing more of value. Yet many were happy that they had survived a war that a good many had paid the price of life. Those who had plenty of food and livestock in their homes before the war found these essentials missing. Chickens and fowls had been stolen by thieves and looters or eaten by the soldiers. Salt and pepper, which were scarce, were among the war casualties also, as well as oil and *gari* and money.

Although the war had ended in Achinva and throughout Ikwerre land, it still raged in the Igbo land and soldiers were still being recruited to fight it. In effect, even though the war had ended for the women and children, for the men it was still raging on. Men were still been sought after to continue the campaign and the assault against Biafra, as what remained unconquered at this time by the Nigerian army were the Biafran strongholds of Orlu, Aba, Abakiliki, Umuahia, Oweri, and the rest.

On the third day after it was announced that the war had ended in Achinva and the villagers were lulled back home by the Nigerian soldiers and the village town crier, the Nigerian soldiers began to capture men in droves.

"You, you, you come here!" a gang of recruiters would say while pointing guns at the men, and the men had no choice in the matter. It was during this unsure period of constant harassment and forced recruitment that a soldier caught Elechi and his friends as they gathered around to talk and reminisce about the war.

"Come with us," they ordered.

"Why?" asked Elechi.

"Ask no questions, just come with us," said Bob Jimmy, a sergeant, and an assistant to the commander of the battalion that still lingered in Achinva village, The Bible.

"Where are we going?" asked Elechi.

"Why are you talking too much? Why not keep quiet like the rest of your friends?" said Bob Jimmy to Elechi.

"But I like to know where I am going?" insisted Elechi.

"Don't worry, we will tell you."

"When?"

"Very soon."

"Why not now?"

"Because we have not decided what we want you to do. Until then, keep your mouth shut," he said. But this was unlike Elechi. He was not used to being told what to do and was not about to begin now. And so when he could not keep him mouth shut, Bob Jimmy ended his life with a lone shot in the chest and sent the rest of the group a very deadly message.

The news of the death of Nwaelechi spread quickly in the village, and along with it the fact that the soldiers were recruiting men to carry their loads of bullets, other ammunitions, and food to the war front and to join in the fighting for the preservation of Nigeria. As such, all able-bodied men in the village were advised to scramble for their lives and to remain hidden in the bushes. Those who had nowhere to hide were told to feign sickness by painting their body with white mud or any form of medicine to show that they were seriously ill and incapacitated and worthless to the Nigerian cause.

When the soldiers discovered what was happening, because the villagers were reporting one another, they took action. It was one

The Victims of Rivalry

of the most despicable and unfortunate incidents of the war, as innocent people turned victims. Some of the women servicing the soldiers and whose husbands had been taken, and who did not want to be the only widows in the village, voluntarily sought out the soldiers and told them what some of the men were doing to evade capture. This, of course, did not please the men, and neither did it please the soldiers. And so the soldiers acted by going door-to-door and asking any man who had smeared anything over his body to take a shower immediately, and in the open, naked, where their children and the world could see them. Those who were caught lying about their sickness were tied hand-to-back with a rope and taken prisoner.

This went on for a whole day, and after they had recruited enough or as many as they could find, the men were ordered to carry the soldiers' foods, ammunitions, and other looted or stolen properties. They then matched towards to borders of Achinva and towards the neighboring villages. And that was the last time many of them were ever seen, dead or alive, by their families. Those who survived this ordeal returned home to recount what they had gone through. One of those lucky men who eventually returned home to his wife and family after over a year of captivity in the warfront was Weneka, the husband of Egbeke and the father of the fortunate twins that set the precedent for preserving twin births in the village of Achinva.

"We were taken to Ndele, to Elele, and then to Owerri, and the rest was history," he recalled as he told the story of his ordeal to Oha Achinike and his council of elders upon returning to the village of Achinva one year later. "We didn't know where we were or where we were going; we just kept walking."

"Why didn't you, or one of you, ask the soldiers where they were taking you?" asked Oha Achinike.

"We could not."

"Why?"

"Well, we all remembered what happened to Elechi. Yet, that knowledge aside, some of us braved it and asked and they were shot immediately and left to rot on the roadside. It was a no-win situation. At some point they would ask us to sit down and rest a while and eat something," he recalled.

"That was all you did."

"I wish. No, that was not all we did. Sometimes they asked us to dig graves for bodies to be buried, and sometimes they asked us to dig trenches for fighting. Many of us died digging those graves and trenches and from starvation and lack of water and proper hygiene," he recalled.

"How did you survive, then?"

"I don't know; I think I was just lucky."

"And the gods and the ancestors were protecting you," added Oha Achinike.

"It must be," said Weneka, "and sometimes I wondered why they did not protect the others," he recalled.

"Well, speak for yourself, young man" said Oha Achinike. "The gods and the ancestors protect justly and they come to the rescue of anyone who calls on them with an open mind. Everybody carries his own *chi* with him or her at all times. When yours is alive, you can survive anything, and when it is dead or angry with you for any reason, your luck will not shine. Yet we cannot blame all misfortune on the gods and the ancestor, just as we cannot heap praises all the time on them for every fortune we meet. You have done well to keep your spirits up and to return home to tell us, despite your ordeal, and we are thankful for your return. We wish others had done the same. We wish they had the same luck. Perhaps they do and will return, just as you did. We will continue to pray and to hope and to wish that they return to us one day soon," concluded Oha Achinike.

All the while he spoke, he poured libations and called on the gods and the ancestors to protect the survivors of the war, whom they had found favors and returned home safely. These men were about ten in number, out of over three hundred men who were matched out of the village of Achinva on that faithless day!

The Victims of Rivalry

Weneka was an important man in the village of Achinva. He was a drummer and a singer and was known for composing some of the most celebrated *eregbu* songs that everyone loved to sing. In fact, when the twin incident happened, he put it in a song that is still sung in the village of Achinva even till this day. The song went like this:

In the eyes of the people of Achinva
children come one at a time.
But in the eyes of God
children come as they please: Some come alone
and others come in pairs.
God gave them to me in pairs,
but the world wanted me to have one.
They speak ill of me
and they speak ill of my wife.
Tears are on my eyes; shame
is on my face.
What does the world want of me: To misspeak and die?
Everyday I sit and wonder what would become
of me
and of my wife
had the white man not spoken
without fear?
Nnadi can speak all they want,
and muckrakers can ridicule me to my face
day and night,
in the hand of Chineke I leave everything.
In his able hands alone,
I surrender everything!

The memory of this song alone brought tears to people's eyes whenever they remembered him, especially when he had not yet returned. And so, in his absence the village mourned and prayed for his return. When finally he returned, the people were overjoyed. Yet not everyone celebrated his comeback. Unfortunately, while he was away and feared dead, which was over one year, his own brother took over his wife and began sleeping with her. While this act was not totally against the custom of the people of Achinva if his brother was truly dead, it must be done through the proper way, which included performing certain rites and rituals necessary for a smooth transfer of one's wife to a brother or a relative. This only happens in the event of death and at the sole discretion of the wife and her family, for she could choose to remarry elsewhere, and to another man, if she does not like the family of her late husband and does not wish to remain there. But out of greed, Weneka's brother, Evuluku, circumvented the law of the land and took in the wife of his absent brother, with the firm belief that his brother had become a casualty of the war.

When Evuluku's secret maneuvers were finally made public, many people voiced their dislike in disgust, but Evuluku would not listen to anyone. Among the first persons to speak up against what they saw as an abomination was Wagbara, the Chief Priest of *Ohiomini*, who was also one of the eldest men in Ordueli family to which Weneka belong.

"What do you think you are doing with Weneka's wife?" he had asked when he ran into the couple in an awkward moment and was desperate for answers, for fear he had witnessed an omen. But the young man dismissed the old man's alarms and fears as unfounded. Later, however, when he was pressured, he decided to lessen the old man's worry and that of the neighbors by agreeing to perform the necessary wife transfer rituals that the gods of the land and the ancestors demanded before he can rightfully posses his brother's wife. But it was too late. He had already slept with her and in her absent husband's bed! In Achinva the tradition holds that a woman who sleeps with another man in her own husband's bed should never live to see another day, unless of course she admits to her crime and agrees to appease the gods and eventually does.

The Victims of Rivalry

Incidentally, however, while the young man was in the midst of preparing for the appeasement rituals, his elder brother, Weneka, returned home alive and well and, as would be expected, eyes rolled over what it saw! Mouths spoke against what the heartfelt. And the gods and the ancestors were not happy! But no one, not even Evuluku, Weneka's brother, himself would venture to tell him what had gone amiss, for fear of what he might do. They didn't have to. Within a fortnight, however, Egbeke, Weneka's wife died, and the war took home yet another victim, a casualty of sort! And Weneka, after learning the truth to his wife's sudden death, did not fail to put his misfortune in a song as he eulogized her, which went like this:

Dear wife,
the marriage we had was good
while it lasted.
The gods have spoken
and the people must obey.
Let it be told that the war took this one
from me, too, along with my pride.
Ah, let it be known to all the world
that a war I know nothing about
took even this one
from me, too.
Let it be said all over the world
that the war took also this part of me
from me, too.
Tears are in my eyes,
Olu-nma,
tears of affection are rolling down my chicks
as I mourn your untimely death.
Let us meet again, soon, Olu-nma,
you and me alone,
let us meet again, soon, very soon
in another world,
one where war and tradition

will not separate us,
ever!
One where we will not become
the casualty
of an unfortunate, sorry war!

As if this anthem of mourning, as it was called then, was not enough, the grieving Weneka followed it up with yet another mournful dirge, which went like this:

I know no one can avert trouble in his life
by prayer alone.
I also know that no one can wish away trouble
even if one wanted to.
But I believe that I have had enough of my share
of troubles and misfortune,
as God and the gods are my witnesses.
Now I am pleading with troubles and misfortune
to please go away,
to please stay away from me
for good.
I am also pleading that they never come my way again
as long as I live!

Not only did this song resonate well because it was coming from Weneka, the man everyone in Achinva now dubbed the first child of misfortune, it also made sense to the entire people of Rumuachinva because it spoke to their collective feelings at the time. It addressed their frustration over a war that shouldn't have been fought in the first place, a war they knew nothing about, and one that disorganized their lives unnecessarily forever!

Chapter 27

The Waterside School Reopened

Few months after the war ended, the Waterside school reopened, but without its founders. Reverend Harcourt did not return, and Mr. Nnadiekwe, his able assistant, was nowhere to be found. He, too, was rumored to have been killed by the Nigerian army. Some of the promising pupils, who had graduated from the school had, for one reason or the other, become casualties of the war. The most profound change, however, was the school's name. It was no longer called The Waterside Missionary School. Instead it its new name became State School Rumuachinva, and this is the name it bears to this day.

The new headmaster of the school, Mr. Daniel Akirika was not well-liked. He was tall and lanky and smoked heavily. He was yellow in complexion and could not look directly into the sun, so he wore glasses, which many thought made him look monstrous and ugly. But he didn't seem to care what people said or thought about him. He went about his business of rebuilding the war-ravaged school with the energy of a youth. He could be seem bouncing from one corner of the school compound to another, and any teacher or pupil who did not follow his order was disciplined indiscriminately. He always walked with a cane in his hand and would not hesitate to use it on any pupil who disobeyed his orders.

Beyond the killing of the two well-educated and promising young men of the village of Achinva, and all the other loses whose census no one took, the most painful loss the village suffered was the loss of too many of her unborn children, her future. Almost all the women who gave birth during the war lost them. No one knew exactly why this occurred, but it did happen. Most died because their mothers were malnourished and had not enough food to feed themselves and their unborn child, so most children were stillborn. Those who were lucky to be born alive had nothing to eat, and, as such, were starved to death, as mothers struggled to survive first.

During the war it was rumored, and rightly so, that Nigeria was intentionally preventing food and other essential goods from reaching Biafra or Eastern Nigeria. As such the stores were empty, and the markets were without goods and food stuffs. Essentials like salt and pepper were severely lacking. As a result people ate saltless and pepperless food, which sometimes caused their stomach to bloat and then run. Disease was rampant, and there were neither doctors nor medicine to cure them. Refugees who had neither bathed nor cleaned themselves in any way smelled like rotten chickens, and these included women and children who had no access to essential hygiene paraphernalia.

At school, children with bulged stomach, which were now known as "kwasiokor" were everywhere. Another sickness called "beriberi" was also common, and the sight of anyone who suffered them, which was quite many, was pitiful. Some looked more ghostlike than human, as they barely had flesh to cover their protruding bones and stomachs. Some were only fat in their bellies—the part of their body where it is obvious their sickness resided. From time to time a truck load of powdered milk arrived at the school compound and each child was given a handful of such delicacies and no more. Whether or not that supplemented the missing essential nutrition, no one knew. All the same, such days were feast days for the children whenever the trucks arrived. Sometimes it was rumored that the Catholic and the Baptist Missionary were coming back to take back the school and that Reverend Harcourt was the one who had sent the powered milk to the school. But when days and months passed and there was no sight of Reverend Harcourt, many hopes dashed and memories of Reverend Harcourt and the good old days faded. But the hopes and the aspirations of the children and the people of Rumuachinva—the victims of this most unfortunate of rivalry—for the bright future of the Nigerian nation, never waned or ceased to gather strength. Today, that hope lives on in the spirit of One—and forward-looking Nigeria!